The Best of Times

My Favourite Football Stories

GEORGE BEST

with

LES SCOTT

Illustrations by David Farris

POCKET
B O O K S

LONDON · SYDNEY · NEW YORK · TOKYO · SINGAPORE · TORONTO

First published in Great Britain by Simon & Schuster UK Ltd,1994
First published by Pocket Books, 1995
This edition published by Pocket Books, 1999
An imprint of Simon & Schuster UK Ltd
A Viacom Company

1 3 5 7 9 10 8 6 4 2

Simon & Schuster UK Ltd
Africa House
64-78 Kingsway
London WC2B 6AH

Simon & Schuster Australia
Sydney

A CIP catalogue record for this book is available from the British Library

ISBN 0-671-03731-5

Printed and bound in Great Britain by Caledonian International
Book Manufacturing, Glasgow

Acknowledgements

Grateful thanks to Mary and Caroline for their help, support and good-humoured encouragement. It speaks volumes that you put up with us both and still have a sense of humour!

Nick Simcock. For research and assistance – only now will those libraries realise the books have gone.

David Farris. For his excellent cartoons – the score draw specialist.

Sean McCarthy of the Holiday Inn Crowne Plaza Midland Hotel, Manchester. Stands to reason that someone who is as long on hospitality as Sean, should come up with such a short and snappy name for his hotel.

Stephen Purdew. For keeping me in shape at Henlow Grange Health Farm.

Steve Shaw at Stillmans Mercedes, Stourbridge. For providing the most stylish wheels on the road.

With special acknowledgement to

Rodney Marsh. Whose memory must be only second to that of the Inland Revenue.

and

Denis Law. For his invaluable contributions. What can one say of a guy who can remember what happened in a dressing room twenty-five years ago, but not whose round it is?

Contents

Fans

The Managers

Directors

The Games

. . . And Now

To Les Scott.

Many, many thanks for all your advice, support and input. Your wonderful sense of humour and considerable knowledge made this book a delight to write. I've never had so many pots of tea and plates of sandwiches in my life!

George Best

London 1994.

Introduction

THERE is a story about how Philip of Macedon realised three ambitions on the same day. He was proclaimed Supreme Victor in the Olympic Games. His wife bore him the son he had always desired and one of his generals defeated a dangerous enemy in battle. Philip, overwhelmed at how fortunate he had been and wondering why he of all people should be singled out for special treatment, is said to have dropped to his knees and prayed to Jove to send him a little misfortune.

Misfortune I can do without, but in many ways I know how Philip of Macedon must have felt. I was born into a hard-working, honest and decent working-class family on the Cregagh Estate in Belfast. I enjoyed my childhood; I listened in lessons, was good at sport, and, as all children do, I dreamed.

I dreamed that one day I would be good enough at football to earn a living from it. To be a professional footballer was my number one ambition and often I would imagine myself in the old gold shirt of Wolverhampton Wanderers, the team I supported from afar as a boy.

I thought if I was not good enough to make it as a footballer, I'd like to work in television or as some sort of entertainer in the theatre. I had no clear idea in my mind of what I would do to entertain – I just liked the idea of doing something that would thrill people or make them smile.

If football, television and the theatre turned out to be

unrealistic ambitions, then I thought writing would be a great way to get by in life.

To become a footballer with the great Manchester United and win League Championship and European Cup winners' medals fulfilled my football ambition beyond my wildest dreams. Now that my footballing days are over, I spend much of my time commentating on the game for television and radio. The theatre shows I do with Rodney Marsh tour the United Kingdom and these nights of fun, laughter and pure football nostalgia go down well with audiences of all ages. All of which left one boyhood ambition unfulfilled: to write a book that captured the great and most entertaining moments of the Golden Age of Football.

In December 1993, I was approached by Les Scott with the idea of compiling a collection of my favourite football stories. The more I talked with Les the more I realised there was a treasure trove of football anecdotes waiting to be told.

We met regularly and as we wallowed in nostalgia, the names, the memories and the stories came flooding back. Les would mention a name or a particular game and it would act as a catalyst to my memory. I began to recall people and incidents I had long since forgotten, such as my chance meeting with the Burnley Chairman Bob Lord, when, in an attempt to flee the press and fans who used to hang around my home in Manchester, I had taken off early one Sunday morning and found myself walking the streets of Burnley; such as the players who were the great characters, like Rodney Marsh, Bobby Keetch, Jimmy Johnstone and Denis Law; the wit and wisdom of managers such as Matt Gillies, Alex Stock, Bill Shankly, Malcolm Allison and the manager most dearest to me, Sir Matt Busby.

When we sat down to write *The Best of Times*, it was a voyage of rediscovery for me: I relived the halcyon days of my time as a player. In so doing I began to realise how important those days were to me in a way that I had never done before. I realised that although I have met more than my fair share of charlatans, deceivers and rip-off merchants, I have also been fortunate enough to have spent time with some of the best people you are ever likely to meet.

Philip of Macedon should have been so lucky. By my reckoning, that is four ambitions realised. I still don't think it warrants a request for a little misfortune, but that's not to say another form of prayer is out of the question.

I was fortunate enough to play football at the highest level with perhaps the greatest club in the world. Here, for the first time, I tell the stories behind the big games, the great characters and some of football's most hilarious moments. Without doubt they were for me, the best of times.

George Best

'94'

Early Days

'There's only one man who can make a man
of you, son – that's you!'

Wilf McGuinness, when youth team coach at Manchester United.

'It's easy to pick out the best young players.
They'll help you do it.'

Bob Bishop, Manchester United scout.

1

Boot Boy to Alex

T HERE were no such things as youth training schemes when I joined Manchester United as a fifteen-year-old in 1961. Young boys were offered an apprenticeship at a football club; after two years your potential to 'make the grade' would be assessed and you would either be offered a professional contract or released from the club.

I was fortunate enough to be offered a professional contract, but the majority of apprentices are not. From a youth team squad of sixteen players, a club would be happy if they had two young lads they thought good enough to merit the offer of a professional contract. The casualty rate for apprentices was high in the early sixties and it is just the same today.

I learned my 'trade' in much the same way as I would have done if I had been serving an apprenticeship as an electrician or engineering fitter. The educational part was punctuated by a lot of menial tasks. Not that I minded – as far as I was concerned it was all part and parcel of a young footballer's life and I loved it.

On Monday mornings my fellow apprentices and I were given brushes, shovels and buckets and told to sweep the terraces. If the first team had been at home the previous Saturday we'd finish at around one o'clock in the afternoon. If the United reserve team, whose average attendance was around 12,000, had played at Old Trafford, we'd finish at around eleven.

My contemporaries as apprentices included wing half John Fitzpatrick, whose collar-length hair was the longest anyone had ever seen at a football club; Willie Anderson, a left winger who many say used me as a role model; David Sadler, a defender who had arrived as a young amateur from Maidstone and with whom I shared digs; John Aston Junior, another winger, who was the son of United's former full back and coach; and Francis Burns, who could play at both full back or wing half. We must have been an exceptional bunch, because we all made it to the United first team and heralded a new era of 'Busby Babes' for United as the new decade got underway.

When we swept the terraces we would pool what we found. Pennies, halfpennies, empty bottles of Corona pop that we could get a penny for if we took them back to the corner shop opposite the Stretford End. The operation over, the spoils would be divided equally between all involved in the clean-up operation.

The apprentices were divided into four groups, each of which would be responsible for cleaning one particular side of the ground. We varied it from week to week, working to a rota system, because in those days you were more likely to find half-crowns in the seats than on the terraces.

Those were the days when the only things that came ready to serve were tennis balls, and after lunch, depending on the time of year, one or two of us might be assigned to groundsman Joe Royle on a Monday afternoon to help him water and tend to the Old Trafford pitch.

Tuesday morning was 'Dubbin Day'. Apprentices were set the task of cleaning all the professionals' boots, which hung in the boot room. Each player had three pegs allocated to him on which he would hang the boots he wore for a match, the boots he trained in and the boots with moulded studs that were used only when the pitches were rock-hard and could not take a conventional stud.

Beneath the pegs would be a small wire cage in which United

players kept, amongst other things, their pumps. In 1961, trainers were people who told us to run around the pitch and not things you wore on your feet. Similarly, coaches were what we travelled to away games on and not advocates of 4–4–2 or 4–3–3 systems of play. When I was an apprentice, the ubiquitous pump-type footwear for footballers was what we called a baseball boot. These were black canvas boots with white laces which came up to a point just above the ankle bone. On the ankle part they had a white rubber disc on which was inscribed, 'The Jets'. Another striking feature of these so-called baseball boots was their white soles, at that time considered most *avant garde*.

We apprentices were each assigned the footwear of two players to look after. I tended to those of goalkeeper Harry Gregg and a centre forward called Alex Dawson, who was later to move on to Preston, for whom he played in the 1964 FA Cup final against West Ham. I don't know why it is, but today when I see photographs of the old pros from that time, they all look so much older than the footballers of today. Alex was no exception. He looked as if he had been born twenty-eight.

Both Harry and Alex were good to me and would tip me a shilling every so often for giving their boots the extra treatment. This was the application of what was called Chelsea Dubbin. Once the boots had been cleaned and polished they looked great, but they were still vulnerable to the mud and wet weather and, in time, the leather would rot and split. That is where dubbin came into its own. I'd rub it on the boots after I'd polished them to make them properly weather and waterproof. The only drawback to this was that dubbin had the effect of making the boots lose their shine. I got around this by rubbing them with vaseline as a finishing touch. It worked a treat – Harry's and Alex's boots shone like glass.

Alex Dawson was a brawny centre forward whose backside was so huge he appeared taller when he sat down. To me, Alex looked like Goliath, although he was only 5 feet 10. What made him such an imposing figure was his girth. He weighed 13 stone 12 pounds, a stone more than centre half Bill Foulkes, who was well over 6 feet tall. What's more, there wasn't an ounce of fat on Alex – it was all muscle. Alex was a Scot from Aberdeen. His parents had moved down to Hull and he had joined United straight from Hull Schoolboys. You didn't argue with him. If it was Tuesday and he told me it was Monday, as far as I was concerned, I'd get back out on the terraces with my sweeping brush.

Apprentices were allowed in to see first-team games free of charge through a special gate that led to the paddock of the main grandstand at Old Trafford. In those days, it was terraced and we stood amongst the United faithful who massed beneath the seated grandstand which rose above and behind us. One night, United were playing Bolton Wanderers in a mid-week, floodlit game, and with minutes remaining, the scores were level at 2–2 when the Bolton goalkeeper Eddie Hopkinson muffed a clearance.

A United attack had broken down and with the ball safe in Hopkinson's hands, the Bolton defenders and the United forwards turned their back on him as they started to make their way up to the halfway line.

But Eddie Hopkinson made a hash of his clearance and instead of the ball sailing deep into the United half of the field, it shot like a bullet to Alex Dawson who, back turned to Hopkinson, was trotting back to the halfway line, blissfully unaware of anything untoward.

The ball hit Alex square on the back of the head like a house brick fired from a cannon. His two crowned front teeth shot from his mouth as he was lifted off his feet and propelled forward. Having hit Alex, the ball bounced off him in the opposite direction and sailed over Eddie Hopkinson, stranded on the edge of his penalty area, and looped into the net.

For a split second the goal was treated with silent disbelief by

the 63,000-strong Old Trafford crowd as they got their heads around the sight they had witnessed. Then the roar went up.

Alex, meanwhile, was lying prostrate, face down on the Old Trafford pitch, legs and arms splayed wide. On hearing the roar, the only movement he made was to raise his right hand six inches off the ground to acknowledge the cheers of the supporters and his score.

The following morning I saw Alex in the boot room. Normally, if a first team player had scored a goal, you would pass the time of day with him by saying, 'Great goal last night', or something like that. In the circumstances, though, this seemed somewhat inappropriate. I busied myself with Alex's boots and sweeping the floor of the boot room as he sat reading a newspaper.

'Aren't you going to say "Well done", for my goal last night?' he asked as I tidied up around him.

I felt very awkward. I couldn't say it was a good goal, because in truth it had been completely farcical, especially as they'd only been able to find one of Alex's front teeth. The search was still on for the other. But I didn't want to anger him, so I decided to compliment him on his scoring. 'Yeah, sorry, Alex. Good goal last night,' I said in a croaky, nervous voice. 'You took it well.' I expected him to correct me and say what a lucky goal it had been.

'Yes, well, when you've been a forward in the game as long as I have been,' he said boastfully, 'you get an instinct for things. In the end, you don't even have to be facing the ball to score!'

2

Awash in Blackpool

From the forties to the late sixties, Blackpool were a footballing force to be reckoned with. As a boy, I marvelled at the skill of the great Stan Matthews as, pin-toed, he displayed his own particular brand of sorcery up and down the touchlines of the First Division.

When I was a boy in Belfast, I remember my dad and his mates debating, seemingly *ad infinitum*, who was the better winger, Stan Matthews or Preston's Tom Finney. Both were English internationals, and both possessed magical ball skills. As far as I can recall, Dad and his pals never resolved the matter – hardly surprising when even the highest court in the land, the House of Lords, baulked at having to make such a decision.

Blackpool teams of the fifties and sixties resembled their own illuminated promenade: full of glitter, razzle, dazzle, interesting side-shows and not without a certain vulgarity. In the fifties, Stan Matthews, centre forward Stan Mortenson and inside forward Ernie Taylor provided the razzle and dazzle, while captain Harry Johnson, Blackpool's right half and hard man, could always be relied on to provide a little vulgarity by way of his sledgehammer tackle.

Matt Busby told me that when Chelsea visited Blackpool's Bloomfield Road ground for a League game in 1955, the Chelsea manager, Ted Drake, had devised a tactic he felt was bound to win the game. It involved the Chelsea inside left, Leslie Stubbs, cutting in from left and taking Harry on his inside. The plan was for Stubbs to draw Johnson towards him and make the Blackpool hard man commit himself to a tackle. Just as Johnson launched himself into the tackle, Stubbs was to slip the ball into the space behind Harry for Chelsea's left half, Derek Saunders, pushing up from deep.

'So I tempt Johnson into the tackle,' said Stubbs, discussing his manager's plan. 'What do you want me to do once Johnson has tackled me?'

'Just try and get better as quickly as you can,' Drake replied with a shrug of the shoulders.

Johnson may well have been the steel in the Blackpool side of that time, but without doubt, Matthews was the catalyst who brought glitzy magic to what, prior to Stan's arrival from Stoke City in 1948, had been a run-of-the-mill team. The rest hung on to his tail and together they sailed over the horizon into a world of Cup finals – they appeared at Wembley in 1948, 1951 and 1953 – and assaults on League Championships. They never actually won the League title, but they were always in the hunt, most notably in 1956, when they were runners-up to Manchester United.

With such a history, it is little wonder that Blackpool held a fascination for me as a young teenager. As I said, I signed for Manchester United in 1961 at the age of fifteen, and my first visit to the famous old seaside town was with the United 'B' team, who were all under sixteen years old and played in Division 2 of the Lancashire League. A year later I returned with the United 'A' team, which played a higher grade of football – in the Lancashire League Division 1!

We were all under seventeen and the 'A' team formed the nucleus of the United team that would compete for the FA Youth Cup, a competition very dear to Matt Busby's heart. The FA Youth Cup had been inaugurated in 1953 and, up to 1961, United had won it five times and reached the semi-finals

14

on the other four occasions. Matt used to think the FA Youth Cup was United's personal property.

In 1962, we were drawn away to Blackpool in the second round of the competition. I was particularly excited about it because the match was to be played at Blackpool's home ground, Bloomfield Road, rather than on their practice ground where the Lancashire League games took place. At last I would tread the very same turf as the great Stanley Matthews!

The game took place in September, and although this would have been late in the season at most seaside resorts, it wasn't the case at Blackpool where everything is geared to the turning on of the illuminations. I'd never seen the illuminations, and having heard that there was plenty of nightlife for a young teenager to enjoy, I was keen to stay over for the night after the game.

Wilf McGuinness was in charge of the United youth team at the time and, along with team-mates David Sadler and John Fitzpatrick, I asked Wilf for permission to stay in Blackpool after the game. Wilf referred the request to Matt Busby. Matt believed young lads would never behave like responsible adults unless they were treated as such, so permission was granted and the club even gave us rail tickets to get back to Manchester.

Wilf gave me the phone number of a guest house and I rang to book in the three of us. The rooms were twin, double and single, so I booked a twin room for David and I and a single for John Fitzpatrick.

We won the game 4–1 against a Blackpool youth team which included a little red-haired winger called Alan Ball, who, at the age of twenty-one, would be part of Alf Ramsey's World Cup-winning team of 1966. Immediately after the game, John, David and I signed ourselves into the guest house and went off looking for the nightlife.

The following morning at breakfast, John Fitzpatrick dropped a bombshell when he told David and me he had spent all his money in the nightclubs and didn't have a bean to pay for his room. David and I had had the good sense to put the money for our room to one side, but apart from that we didn't have an extra penny between us, either. In 1962, Access was something the police gained when they went visiting, and Visa a piece of paper you needed when you visited the USA. Over breakfast, we debated what we could do about the bill for John's room.

David suggested ringing Wilf McGuinness and asking if United could take care of the outstanding bill if John could pay it back when he could afford to. I reminded David about Matt's viewpoint. What John had done was hardly the mark of a responsible adult and the boss might put the kybosh on any future requests to stay over after games.

We were in a quandary. Eventually I suggested that the only way around the problem was for John to do a runner. As we did not have to vacate the rooms until eleven in the morning. I suggested that at around ten o'clock, David and I should settle our bill and check out of the guest house. We could have John's clothes in our overnight bag and five minutes after we had left, John could come down from his room wearing his swimming trunks and carrying a towel as if he were going for a quick swim. The plan was to give the landlady the impression that John would check out and settle his bill once he had returned from his dip. Having left the guest house in his swimming trunks, John would then join David and me a few hundred yards along the prom, where he would change into his clothes and the three of us would head back to Manchester.

The plan worked liked a dream. The landlady never suspected a thing as John presented himself in the foyer in his swimming trunks and we got away without John having to pay.

But that prank preyed on our conscience. We felt bad about it because the lady who ran the guest house had been so kind and friendly. So, two years later, when Manchester United played Blackpool in the First Division and David, John and I were all in the side, we decided to find the guest house and make it up to

16

the landlady. United had booked into a hotel on the promenade for a pre-match meal and as the rest of the players relaxed for an hour or so before departing for the game, John Fitzpatrick and I set off to buy the biggest bunch of flowers we could find. We thought if John paid a bit on top of what was owed on the room and presented the landlady with flowers and chocolates, we might just be forgiven for pulling such a mean trick.

Flowers and chocolates in hand, John rang the doorbell of the guest house. We saw the outline of our landlady through the frosted glass in the door as she came along the hall to answer it. As the she opened the door, John beamed a smile and thrust the bunch of flowers towards her. She studied his face for a second or two then let forth a piercing scream before falling against the wall and slithering to the floor in a faint.

John and I stood dumbfounded as her husband ran to her aid and tried to revive her. As he gently splashed water on his wife's face, he peered up at John Fitzpatrick and gave him a look as black as thunder.

'You stupid young bugger!' he shouted. 'We thought you'd drowned!'

3

The Debuts

MANCHESTER UNITED had a scout in Northern Ireland called Bob Bishop, and it was he who discovered me. Bishop had seen me play schools football and in 1961 he sent a telegram to Matt Busby which said: 'I believe I've found you a genius.'

Bob Bishop was very highly thought of by Matt and he wasted no time in bringing me over to Manchester. I had never travelled more than fifteen miles from Belfast and Manchester seemed like the other side of the world. Like a poor wine, I didn't travel well. I had never even worn long trousers before so my mother bought me a pair because she felt I would be the butt of everyone's jokes if I turned up in short trousers for my first job! I travelled across the Irish Sea with a boy called Eric McMordie who, like me, would return, homesick, to Belfast within twenty-four hours of arriving in Manchester.

I was unsure of myself as a player then. I did not believe I was good enough to make the grade as a footballer, especially at a big club like United, which I found very intimidating. After all, the Irish clubs had watched me play schools football and none of them had wanted to sign me. If I wasn't good enough for them, how could I possibly be good enough for a club like Manchester United?

Journeying back to Belfast, I told Eric McMordie that I didn't think I was cut out to be a footballer because I wasn't good enough. Eric said he still wanted to be a footballer, but not in a place like Manchester. He wanted to sign for a club surrounded by lovely countryside and next to a beautiful bay. He was, he told me, a country boy at heart and would only sign for someone like Cobh Rangers in the Irish League.

I returned to Manchester United to become one of their most celebrated players. Eric, too, went back to England – and signed for Middlesbrough!

Matt Busby spoke to my father on the telephone and he asked Matt to take me back, which he agreed to do. Matt understood my anxieties and told the United coaching staff, 'Don't tinker with the boy's style. Let him develop his own way, naturally. I believe he's something special.' I was grateful even then for Matt's careful nurturing.

My first wage was £4 1s 9d, of which I sent £3 back to my mum to help towards the family. That left me with £1 1s 9d – the Equivalent of £1.09 – which for a kid from a Belfast council estate seemed a lot.

As I settled in, my confidence began to grow and in 1962 I made it into the United reserve team for the first time for a game against West Bromwich Albion in the Central League. I was playing outside right and was up against West Brom's regular first team left back, Graham Williams, who was having a run-out in the reserves following an injury. Williams was a Welsh international, a seasoned First Division player and one who relished his reputation for eating young players like me for breakfast. He had short, cropped hair and his upper torso was shaped like a lightbulb compared to his waist. Williams possessed the most muscular legs I had ever seen and they protruded from his shorts like bags of concrete. I could have wished for an easier debut.

As it turned out, that game against West Brom reserves and Williams was the first of three amazing coincidences for me. A year later, in mid-September 1963, I was picked to make my first-team debut in place of the regular first-team winger, Ian

Moir, who was injured. The game took place at Old Trafford against West Bromwich Albion and the full back marking me was, once again, Graham Williams.

I felt I gave a good account of myself in a 1–0 win. The report in the *Manchester Pink Final* read: 'Young Best often showed Albion's international full back Williams a clean pair of heels.' I was so excited I read it again and again and bought extra copies to send home to my family in Belfast.

Some months later, I received a late call-up for the Northern Ireland squad for an international against Wales at Vetch Field, the home of Swansea Town, as they were then called. In truth, I didn't expect to play as I was only just eighteen, and it came as quite a surprise to me when I was told I had been picked at outside right.

When I took to the field for my international debut I looked across the pitch to see who would be marking me. It was none other than Graham Williams.

That Welsh team included Gary Sprake of Leeds United in goal, Mike England of Blackburn Rovers, Barry Jones of Plymouth Argyle, Ron Davies of Southampton and Cliff Jones, who had played for Spurs in the double-winning side of 1960–61. They appeared to me to be a vastly experienced side compared to Northern Ireland.

I wasn't the only boy making his international debut that day. In goal for Northern Ireland was a young goalkeeper from Watford by the name of Pat Jennings, who, of course, would go on to find fame and fortune with Spurs and Arsenal and win a record 119 caps for his country.

We won the game 3–2 with goals from Sunderland's Martin Harvey, Sammy Wilson of Falkirk and, ironically, Jim McLaughlin, who played for Swansea. During the after-match buffet for the players I was feeling particularly pleased with myself because I knew I had had a good game, and what was more I had set up two of our three goals. I was standing by myself with a plate of sandwiches in the players' lounge when I noticed Graham Williams enter the room.

He made a point of glancing around as if looking for someone. Only when his eyes met mine did I start to worry. I watched in mounting terror as the big Welsh full back made a beeline for me. His eyes were expressionless like those of a shark and his tall frame erect as a Grecian pillar. I began to feel very uneasy, but I had nowhere to escape. As Williams reached me he raised two hands the size of shovels and gripped both sides of my face. I let my plate of sandwiches fall to the floor as I feared the worst. He held my head in his hands and thrust his face to within inches from mine.

'So that's what your face looks like', he said. 'I had to come and look because I've played against you three times now and all I've ever seen of you is your bloody arse.' And with that, he extended a hand of friendship – which, I don't mind telling you, I was only too glad to shake.

4

Long Memory

D URING the 1964–65 season, Manchester United ventured into Europe once again when they won a place in the Fairs Cup, later renamed the UEFA Cup.

I had made my European debut the previous year when, as a seventeen-year-old, I played for United against Sporting Lisbon in the quarter-final of the European Cup-Winners' Cup. My debut was a bitter-sweet experience, for having won the first leg 4–1 at Old Trafford, we contrived to lose the away leg 0–5 and consequently went out 4–6 on aggregate. We underestimated the strength of Sporting, who went on to win the trophy. Sporting had knocked out the Italian side Atalanta in the first round and then beaten Apoel Nicosia by the not inconsequential score of 16–1 in the first leg of round two. I remember our coach, Wilf McGuinness, returning from Lisbon having watched that game and telling Matt Busby, 'It was an even game. They scored eight in each half.' Having lost to Sporting the previous year made us even more determined to do well in the Fairs Cup, and after drawing 1–1 in the first round against the Swedish side Djurgaarden, we cantered home at Old Trafford by 6–1.

Confidence was high and even when we drew the top West German side Borussia Dortmund in the following round, we felt our chances of further progress were good. The first leg was in Dortmund and we literally played them off the park. Bobby Charlton controlled the game from midfield, Denis Law was in top form and we were the winners, again by 6–1. The home leg became a formality.

What I remember most about that trip to Dortmund is sitting in the hotel TV lounge with the rest of the team watching the Frank Sinatra film *The Manchurian Candidate*. The film was in English with German subtitles. All the United players were gathered around the hotel TV set watching the film the night before we were due to play Dortmund. Amongst us were centre half Bill Foulkes and goalkeeper Dave Gaskell.

Bill and Dave had for some days indulged in a betting frenzy which was well over the top. They'd reached the stage where they would literally bet on anything. They sat on the team bus and bet sixpence that I'd be the next person to board it. They bet on what colour tie Matt Busby would wear that day or on whether Shay Brennan would start his meal by eating part of his bread roll or with a mouthful of soup. They had gone betting mad.

In *The Manchurian Candidate*, there is a scene where Frank Sinatra checks into a hotel carrying a briefcase containing secret papers which have evidence about the brain-washing of American POWs in North Korea. Sinatra places the briefcase on the floor of the hotel reception area as he prepares to check in. As he's signing the register, a woman comes alongside him and places an identical briefcase on the ground next to his.

'Bet you ten bob Sinatra picks up the wrong briefcase,' Big Bill said to young Dave.

'You're on.'

We all watched as Frank Sinatra duly obliged Bill, turning, picking up the woman's suitcase and heading off towards his room. The woman, deciding not to sign in at the hotel, picks up the briefcase with the damning information and heads off into the street.

Dave Gaskell thrust his hand into his pocket to a chorus of

'You must have more money than sense,' from the rest of us and handed Big Bill a ten-bob note.

After fifteen minutes or so, Bill, who was sitting on one of the armchairs, leaned forward to Dave, seated cross-legged on the floor. 'Here. Take this back.'

'No fear. A bet's a bet,' Dave said, waving away the proffered ten-bob note.

'Take it back,' Bill insisted. 'I can't take it from you.'

'Why not?'

'Because I knew Sinatra would pick up the wrong briefcase. I've seen this film before.' Bill confessed.

'That's OK,' said Dave. 'So have I. Keep the money.'

A few seconds passed. Bill was a big, brawny centre half, not noted for great intellectual prowess, though nevertheless credited with more grey cells than young Dave. Perhaps it just didn't occur to Bill, but I felt I had to ask the question I was sure would be on the minds of most of the other players.

'If you've seen this film before, Dave,' I asked, 'Then why the hell did you bet that Sinatra would pick up the wrong briefcase?'

'Because I didn't think he'd be daft enough to make the same mistake twice!' he said as the room erupted with laughter.

'I don't friggin' believe it!' shouted Denis, honking with mirth and slapping both knees with his hands. 'Is this guy serious?'

Dave was. A very competent goalkeeper, he was, unwittingly, an endless source of amusement at United. In one hotel, when ordering a soup starter, he informed the waiter that he'd have 'the mine-strown soup'. On another occasion, in Spain, during a pre-season tour, he was served with *gazpacho*. Denis Law and Nobby Stiles pretended their *gazpacho* was hot and told Dave to complain to the hotel manager when he, of course, reported that his was stone-cold.

In the same season, after a home game against Spurs, Denis Law was dressing after his shower and discovered that the toes of his socks and the sleeves of his shirt had been cut off. Unsurprisingly, Denis wanted to know who had done it. At first no one would tell, but eventually one or two of us nodded towards Dave Gaskell's peg. Denis filled trainer Jack Crompton's bucket with ice-cold water and threw two whole bucketfuls over a screaming Dave, still in the bath.

When Dave emerged, he demanded to know where Denis had gone and we pointed towards one of the toilet cubicles. Nobby Stiles and I egged him on to give Denis a taste of his own medicine. He didn't need much persuading. Standing on the loo seat of the next-door cubicle, Dave emptied a bucket of cold water over Denis as he sat reading a newspaper on the loo.

When Denis came back into the changing room, the suit he was wearing was soaked through. Dave was beside himself with laughter.

Denis calmly went across to his peg, removed the suit and shirt he was wearing, placed them on the phsyio's bench, towelled himself down, then took his own shirt with the cut-off sleeves and another pristine suit from his peg and put them on. I can still picture Dave Gaskell's face to this day when he cottoned on that Denis had in fact been wearing *his* suit in the toilet cubicle. Mouth gaping, he stood for half a minute staring in disbelief.

It was all lighthearted, taken in good part, and it was what made life at United such great fun. The atmosphere was terrific. We were like one big family. If you played practical jokes on a team-mate or wound him up, you simply had to take it and not sulk when he got back at you.

The return leg against Borussia Dortmund was a cinch. As they had lost the first leg to us 1–6, I thought the Germans would be tougher opposition at Old Trafford. I believed they would want to prove they were not as bad a side as the first score suggested and consequently would have their pride to play for. But we

ran out 4–0 winners, making it 10–1 on aggregate. In truth, if we had really pushed it, I reckon we could have won by ten on the night.

We were 2–0 up at half-time, and as the two teams walked off the pitch I followed three Dortmund players towards the tunnel leading to the dressing rooms. At the entrance I noticed a supporter in his late sixties. He was wearing a red and white woollen United bobble hat and muffler and leaning over the wall. He reached out his left arm and I thought he was preparing to pat me on the back as I made my way past him and into the tunnel. But just as the three Dortmund players were about to walk past him, the old man waved a clenched fist at them, cackling, 'That'll teach you to bomb our house!'

5

Willie's Woe

TRAINING at the Cliff would inevitably end with small games of four or five a side. Assistant manager Jimmy Murphy would erect small posts, or simply place traffic cones around the practice pitches, and two or three games would immediately get underway.

These games were immense fun and would involve three basic rules of play. If Jimmy shouted, 'Open!', the players would play as in a proper game. On receiving the ball we'd have as much contact with it as we liked. When Jimmy called out 'One' or 'Two', however, it told us how many times we were allowed contact with the ball before passing or shooting. The thing about one or two-touch football is that it helps your control. There is no margin for error and it quickens the pace of a game. In essence, it makes you a better player by improving your first touch – essential if you are to play at the highest level. Touching the ball more times than you were allowed, incurred a punishment of press-ups and a barrage of good-humoured derision from team-mates.

More often than not the management would form themselves into a team that would include Jimmy, coach Wilf McGuinness and occasionally Matt Busby himself. The difference between a side comprised of players and the management team was that the management team took these games very seriously. It was their only opportunity to play an organised game of football themselves and they would put as much energy into it as if they were playing at Wembley in a Cup final. So, if your five-a-side team was selected to play against the management, you knew you were in for a highly competitive contest where no quarter would be asked or given.

One day a side comprising the likes of Denis Law, John Fitzpatrick and Nobby Stiles was involved in a battle royal with Jimmy Murphy's management team. The first team to score five goals were the winners, and the game in which I was involved had finished. I began making my way back to the Cliff changing room with Willie Anderson, who, like me, was a winger.

Willie was a very sharp and tricky player whose number of first-team appearances had been restricted due to the form of myself and John Aston, who played out wide on the left. The magic and charisma of Manchester United is a heady mixture and it kept Willie at Old Trafford, even though he spent the majority of his seasons in the reserves. I always believed he would have walked into any other First Division side at the time, but instead he waited in the wings for a chance to establish himself as a first-team regular.

Eventually, Willie realised that his career was slipping away and, not wanting to spend it in the Central League with the reserves, he asked for a move. Aston Villa snapped him up and he went on to give them sterling service in keeping with the good professional he was.

Some say Willie modelled himself on me. I don't know about that, but he did grow his hair long and wear it in a style similar to mine. There were a number of other similarities in our styles of play, but there was one big difference: Willie was a very quiet, shy and unassuming lad. He hardly ever spoke in the dressing room and would change, play, shower and leave the ground without speaking more than a few sentences all the time he was there. Don't get me wrong, Willie wasn't dull or boring, just very quiet. On those occasions when I did engage him in conversation, he proved to be quite knowledgeable and revealed a wit as dry as the Gobi desert.

On our way back for a shower, Willie and I took time out to watch what was a highly contested and niggling game between Denis's side and the management. The management were on the attack when suddenly the ball broke to Jimmy Murphy, who shot for goal.

It was difficult to say whether Jimmy had scored or not because the ball flashed over the top of one of the traffic cones they were using as a post. The management team whooped and cheered, convinced they had won the game.

'OK, that's it. Five-four. In we go.' Jimmy shouted, pointing towards the changing rooms.

'That was never a goal!' Denis protested.

'Course it was. Must have been a foot goal-side of the cone!' retorted Wilf McGuinness.

'I was right by it. The ball went the other side of the cone. It missed by a mile,' claimed Nobby.

'It was a goal, I tell you!' Jimmy said, getting a little worked up.

'Never was!' Denis replied, standing his ground.

Willie and I stood looking on as one hell of an argument erupted. Nobby Stiles placed the ball on the ground to take a goal-kick, only for Jimmy to pick it up and order everyone into the changing room. Denis and his team refused to go, arguing more vehemently than ever that Jimmy's shot had gone wide. The row raged for three or four minutes and was in full flow when Matt Busby appeared, demanding to know what it was all about. On being told, Matt, ever the diplomat, put forward a solution. 'Let's take an unbiased opinion,' he said, turning towards Willie and me. 'Did you see Jimmy's shot, Willie?' he asked.

'Yes,' Willie said softly.

'And?' Matt asked, looking for a decision.

Willie stood uncomfortably for a few moments.

'Come on. Don't be afraid to tell us what you saw,' said Matt encouragingly.

'Well, to be perfectly honest,' Willie said nervously, 'I thought it missed.'

'Well, there we go! Game continues,' Matt said triumphantly.

Willie and I made our way to the changing rooms and before long, Denis's team entered, full of themselves at having eventually beaten the management 5–4. Seconds later, the changing room door was thrown open with such violence that it nearly came off its hinges. A seething Jimmy Murphy entered and made his way across to a petrified Willie Anderson. 'You little bastard!' he roared. 'You've been at this club for five years and never said boo to a goose. And when you do finally open your mouth to speak, it's a bloody lie!'

The Players

'He's a dinghy player. When the ship starts
to sink he's the first to leave it.'

Harry Catterick, former Everton manager.

'Genius has its limitations, George. But
stupidity has no such handicaps.'

Denis Law, former Manchester United player.

6

Rodney Marsh

RODNEY MARSH is one of my closest friends. Like me, he has always believed in entertaining football played in a swashbuckling, cavalier manner. During his time at Fulham, QPR and Manchester City he put into practice what he preached.

I had the good fortune to play with Rodney when he was in his second spell at Fulham in 1976. As a footballer he was a showman with an impish streak, a ball-juggler extraordinaire. The best part of his career was a continuous aggravation and affront to the conventional.

On and off the field, Rodney was incalculable and outrageous. Eccentric, somewhat erratic, he was a highly gifted individualist whose nine caps for England was meagre reward for talent in abundance. Rodney also has courage aplenty. As a teenager with Fulham he had the hearing kicked out of one ear as he threw himself across the ground to head a spectacular goal. Hence his outwardly engaging, but inwardly pained habit of tilting his head to one side during conversation.

Rodney was always willing to try something different and was a delight to watch on the football field. In the early sixties, when he first signed for Fulham, he played for the reserves in a Football Combination match against Birmingham City reserves.

The Fulham goalkeeper, Ken Hewkins, sustained an injury

and was stretchered off the field. Rodney volunteered to go in goal. A few minutes later, Birmingham won a corner on the Fulham left. The City winger Mike Hellawell took the corner and as the ball came over near to the crossbar, Rodney tried to send it over the top with a flying bicycle kick. Own goal.

'What the hell were you trying to do out there?' the Fulham manager, Bedford Jezzard, asked.

'Entertain,' said young Rodney.

'If I wanted players to go out on to the pitch and entertain, I'd go to Billy Smart's and sign two clowns!' said Jezzard.

'You've got a first team full of them, what do you want two more for?' Rodney asked.

Two weeks later, in search of greater appreciation of his extravagant skills, Rodney transferred across west London to Queen's Park Rangers. At Loftus Road he was worshipped by the fans, respected by his team-mates and admired by Alex Stock, the manager who took him there. 'So you think you can play football and entertain out there on the pitch?' asked Stock.

'Yes.' said Rodney.

'Then don't let me stop you. Express yourself. Make the fans leave this ground excited about what they've seen. Send them home with the feeling that football is a wonderful game after all and a wonderfully clever one at that. Do that and they'll be back in their droves and they'll bring their friends with them.'

Rodney carried out his manager's wishes to the letter. He didn't just entertain the fans, he astonished them. Stock was right – the Rangers supporters loved Rodney's style of play. Attendances at Queen's Park Rangers in the mid-sixties jumped from an average of 8,000 in 1965 to 22,000 in 1968. They won promotion from Division 3 to Division 1 and won the League Cup at Wembley in 1967 with a flamboyant and stylish 3–2 victory over First Division West Bromwich Albion.

It was all achieved with a wonderful, fun-loving spirit permeating the club at all levels. On the pitch, Rodney was still up to his tricks, but this time with the blessing of his manager. For the best part of a game, Rodney would put on a masterly show of midfield play which no player at the time could equal. Positive and unselfish, he would direct play until such time as he felt his team had a comfortable lead. Then he would decide he had had enough of hard graft and discipline for one afternoon and set about amusing himself and giving the fans their memories.

Against Birmingham City, in 1968, he scored a superb hat-trick in a 3–0 victory, a feat that ITV commentator Brian Moore tells me is one of the best hat-tricks he has ever seen. Brimming with confidence, Rodney found himself out on the left touchline in space with the ball. Putting his right foot on the ball, he looked at his left wrist as if he was checking the time on a watch. As the Birmingham defender, Roger Hynd, closed in on him, Rodney pointed to his imaginary watch and tapped his wrist with a finger, indicating that it was time for him to go, and took off once again towards the City goal. The crowd went beserk. They loved it.

In 1970, against Newcastle United, Rodney weaved his way through a maze of black and white shirts, every swerve and feint, jink and dodge producing a fresh roar of approval from those assembled. Eventually, there was only the Newcastle goalkeeper, Iam McFaul, to beat. Rodney swept past him, and with the goal gaping at his mercy, took the ball forward and stopped it on the line. As the Newcastle defender Bob Moncur sprinted towards the goal, Rodney called out: 'Hurry up, Bob, it's not over the line yet, you just might catch it.' Goal!

Following that game, a reporter for a Sunday colour supplement who was doing a piece on Rodney began by asking him if he had had a happy childhood. 'I am still having a happy childhood,' he replied.

Outside the confines of west London there were few who were convinced that here was a talent which could be as profound as it was exciting. One person who did recognise Rodney's true genius was Manchester City coach Malcolm Allison, who had the confidence in his ability to offer him the larger stage of one of England's major clubs.

One of his nine caps for England was gained at Wembley against West Germany in 1971. Rodney was disappointed to have been named as a substitute and was far from his usual bubbly, ebullient self as the team prepared for the game in the home dressing room.

Manager Sir Alf Ramsey delivered his team talk and ended by asking who wanted to take penalties should England be awarded any. No one spoke. 'Colin, what about you?' he asked Colin Bell of Manchester City.

Bell shook his head.

He turned to Martin Chivers. 'Fancy stepping up to take a penalty if we get one, Martin?' The big centre forward from Spurs declined.

'Emlyn, penalties?' Ramsey continued.

Emlyn Hughes of Liverpool said he'd be much happier if someone else took them.

Ramsey surveyed the room. His eyes paused at Rodney. 'Rodney, surely you have the confidence to put a penalty away at Wembley?' Ramsey said hopefully.

'Sure. Wouldn't bother me at all.' Rodney said.

'Great! That's settled, then. If we get a penalty, Rodney's going to be our man,' Ramsey said, rubbing his hands together.

Rodney raised his right arm. 'Only one little problem, Alf.'

'And what's that?' Ramsey asked in his cultured voice.

'You didn't bloody well pick me for the team!'

It is stories such as these that made Rodney and I decide to name the theatre tours we do together 'A Football Night to Remember', and not 'How to Win Friends and Influence People'.

7

After a Fashion

THE seventies began with my hair over the collar and making a valiant effort to come to rest on my shoulders. My trousers had enough flare to rig an East India-bound clipper and my tie a knot the size of a small cushion.

I cut a dash around the bars of Manchester in shoes the size of divers' boots. When they wore out I didn't bother to get them soled or heeled, but if I had done, it would have been more appropriate to take them to Cammel Laird Dry Dock than to a cobbler's. The gear I sported in the seventies was anything but minimalist.

By the end of the decade, fashion had changed considerably, likewise football. The seventies began with an air of naivety. The game was there to be enjoyed. I still thought it fun to play. It ended with cynicism rife both on and off the pitch. The seventies saw the first seeds of football commercialism being planted in highly fertile ground. At first football's administrators played and tinkered with it, knowing there was a vast reservoir of oil to be tapped but unable to hit upon the right way to get it. It gave rise in the seventies to the Watney Cup, the Anglo-Scottish Cup, the Texaco Cup and, unbelievably, in 1977, the Debenhams Cup. All different competitions and each firing players and fans with about as much enthusiasm and interest as watching a fish finger defrost.

Alan Hardaker's People's Cup, which was launched in 1960,

was still known simply as the League Cup. Since 1967, the final had been staged at Wembley rather than as a two-legged affair played at the home grounds of the two competing finalists. In the seventies, the Wembley final was staged on a Saturday afternoon when a full programme of Football League fixtures was taking place. It was as if all the clubs which had failed to reach the final were behaving as if they had never wanted to get to Wembley in the first place. Shunned, the two finalists were left to throw their own private party.

The England team under Don Revie cautiously embraced commercialism in 1974. A contract was made with sports equipment manufacturers Admiral and the first items to have the manufacturer's logo emblazoned on them were the towels used by the England team. Rodney Marsh used to say, 'We'll only get to see the towel logo when Revie throws one in' – which, eventually, he did.

Not long afterwards, the England team broke with tradition by sporting the Admiral crest on their shirts and red and blue stripes down their sleeves. The days when a boy could wear a white T-shirt, a blue pair of shorts and a white pair of socks and think he had the England strip were over.

Derby County were one of the first clubs to press for sponsors logos on shirt-fronts. Soon Sony, Crown Paints and the local DIY store were as much a part of the club strip as its badge. Today, football strips are fashion accessories. The marketing moguls, not content to change the strip on an annual basis, introduce sometimes up to three different kits a season to drain every last penny from the fans. Goalkeepers' tops look as if they were designed by Julian Clary with a migraine. Some may say it's a natural progression which has added much-needed colour to football. All I can say is that it wasn't necessary to add artificial colour to the game in the sixties or early seventies – there were plenty of characters on the pitch to ensure that the game was colourful enough on its own.

THIS WEEK'S KIT OUT NOW! TELL YOUR FOLKS!

Players such as Denis Law, Rodney Marsh, Stan Bowles, Tony Currie, Kevin Keegan and Alan Hudson readily come to mind; players who could produce the unexpected. A touch of genius and individual flair that would send a crowd into raptures and David Coleman or Barry Davies into apoplexy. They are all favourites of mine, because they entertained and made football fun.

There were others: Terry Mancini of QPR, Orient and Arsenal, for example. When he was at QPR, in 1974, he had such a run of scoring own goals that his own centre forward, Don Givens, used to drop back and mark him every time they conceded a corner. I played against him in 1970 when he was at Leyton Orient. As the Orient and United teams took the field I found myself next to Terry, who had a reputation as a fearsome tackler. 'Don't look so worried, George,' he said. 'I'm in a humane mood today. I've put iodine on my studs.'

Then there was Chico Hamilton, who joined Aston Villa from Southend. On being told that a home defeat by Liverpool had put Villa, who had a poor side at the time, bottom of the League, he said resolutely, 'Yes, and we'll take some shifting.'

Don Masson of Notts County was a highly gifted and entertaining, if unsung, midfield player. In 1973, against Portsmouth at Fratton Park, Don, Kevin Randall and Brian Stubbs all missed penalties for County. With seconds remaining, County's Les Bradd cut into the Pompey penalty area only to be brought down by Paul Went, the home centre half. As the referee raised his arm, Don caught hold of his hand and prevented him from whistling for the spot kick. 'We don't want it,' Don told the bemused official. 'We've missed three already and the fans think we're prats enough as it is!'

One of my Manchester pals was also a highly entertaining player in his time – and before I get accused of being too pro-United, let me say that he played for City. Denis Tueart won an FA Youth Cup-winners' medal with Sunderland and the nucleus of that side went on to win one of the most famous Wembley finals of all time: when still in the Second Division, Sunderland beat the mighty Leeds United in the 1973 FA Cup final. Sunderland's failure to win promotion the following season made the likes of Tueart and Mick Horswill yearn for First Division football. Which is why, when Manchester City came in with an offer for both of them, they jumped at the chance.

Denis was a skilful, lively front player who liked to improvise his considerable talents out wide. He carried an air of easy glamour and on his day could be as electric and bewitching as the best wingers, combining pace with grace. When confronted with a full back he'd side-step him as easily as he might avoid someone standing in his way on the pavement. His repertoire was considerable and if you were to compare him with, say, John Barnes, Barnes would be the enigma without variation.

Like his former wing partner at Sunderland, Billy Hughes, he loved to cut inside and have a go. On those odd occasions when he sent a shot up into the terraces, there would be no swearing, grimacing and stamping of the foot. Denis would simply stand, hands on hips, eyes following the trajectory of the ball. He'd shake his head in wonderment at his folly, smile to himself then take to his toes to regain his position. Whether you played on the same pitch as Denis or watched him from the terraces, you were left in no doubt that he enjoyed his game and loved to provide the fans with something spectacular. Who can forget his overhead bicycle kick to score the winning goal for City against Newcastle United in the League Cup final of 1976?

Denis quickly established himself in a City team that could boast the likes of Colin Bell, Francis Lee, Tommy Booth, Willie Donachie, Mike Summerbee and a certain Denis Law. In the mid-seventies City were managed by Tony Book and his assistant and coach was Ian McFarlane. City's home record was impressive and one home defeat in a season was rare. In

1974–75 they did, however, suffer two home losses, one to Derby County and the other, rather surprisingly, to Carlisle, who were to be relegated that season after one year in the First Division.

At half-time against Carlisle the scores were level and there was everything to play for. At such times, you expect the management to offer words of encouragement and advice, perhaps to chide you for being a little over-cautious and encourage you to 'have a go' at the opposition whilst extolling your attributes as a player. Not so McFarlane.

The perspiring players were sitting around the dressing room, staring at their boots and seemingly on autopilot as they sipped their tea, when McFarlane entered the room. Almost at once he launched into a tirade of abuse that would have had Bernard Manning wincing with embarrassment. Running them down and telling them just how awful they were as individuals and as a team, McFarlane offered them his own personal brand of sledging. The players sat in silence and took it all.

Just when it seemed that McFarlane had finished, he'd start again. The players glanced at each another as they sought reassurance amongst themselves. McFarlane had not only gone over the top but was also out of order. It was a Basil Fawlty performance and the players began to wonder whether he had lost his marbles. After six or seven minutes of invective and rebuke, McFarlane rounded up by telling the players that they had 'served up the biggest heap of crap' – he had ever seen on a football field.

No one spoke. No one shuffled. All sat silent and still. Suddenly, a throat was cleared as a player prepared to speak. 'Well, I don't think we've played all that badly,' said Denis Tueart in all earnestness.

McFarlane didn't say a word. He simply swung around, leaned back slightly, wound up his right arm and threw a fist the size of a ham shank at Denis. It connected with full-blast

46

force with his cheekbone. Denis's head jerked back violently, bounced off the wall behind him and immediately began to swell, his face turning redder than a rose.

All eyes went to Denis, then to McFarlane. The room was silent but the tension was like a piano wire. Suddenly, the buzzer sounded indicating that the players should take the field for the second half. They filed past McFarlane as though he were a serial killer.

As they made their way down the tunnel, Denis walked alongside Rodney Marsh and wiped a trickle of blood from the corner of his mouth with the sleeve of his shirt. 'When things are not going so well on the pitch,' he said to Rodney, 'you can always depend on that guy to get the worst out of you.'

On hearing of the incident, one of Denis's friends persuaded him to take legal advice on the matter. Denis made an appointment with a solicitor in Manchester who happened to be a City season-ticket holder. Denis told him what had happened and the solicitor sat in silence with a dour expression on his face. 'And who were you playing when this incident took place at half-time?' he asked.

'Carlisle United,' said Denis.

For a few seconds there was silence as the solicitor stared at him with an expressionless face. 'I remember the way you played that day. If I could have got to you, I would have hit you as well,' he said, and bade Denis good day.

8

The Charltons

M Y old team-mate Bobby Charlton and his brother Jack, the current manager of the Republic of Ireland, are, to my mind, the most famous of all footballing brothers. Both enjoyed very successful careers, Bobby with United and Jack with Leeds, and both, of course, were members of the England team that won the World Cup in 1966. Whilst Jack is still involved in the game, nowadays Bobby runs a successful sports promotion company.

In their playing days, I think it is fair to say that Bobby enjoyed more of a glamorous reputation than Jack. Then, as now, neither brother resented the other's success and to my knowledge there has never been any jealousy between soccer's most celebrated siblings. I do recall, however, one incident that rankled with Jack, although it had nothing directly to do with Bobby. It involved a wonderful man called Sam Leitch, who was a journalist with the *Sunday Mirror* and BBC TV.

Manchester United had played Leeds in a match at Elland Road in 1967 and Sam, having submitted his copy to his editor, came into the players' lounge for a drink. Noticing Big Jack enjoying a quiet pint on his own in a corner, he went up to pass the time of day. 'Hello, Jack,' he said.

'Hello Sam.'

'How's your Bobby?'

Jack slammed his pint down on the table. 'Do you

know what really gets to me about you, Sam?' he said tersely.

'No,' replied Sam, somewhat taken aback.

'Every time you see me, you always ask how our kid is. That's fine. But not once do you ever ask me how I am.' said Jack, peeved. 'I'm always seeing you after matches and it's always Bobby, Bobby, Bobby with you. I'm an individual in my own right, you know, not just Bobby Charlton's brother. Ask me how I am for a change!'

Sam Leitch gently settled his portly frame on the seat next to Jack. 'I'm sorry, Jack,' he said sympathetically. 'I never realised you felt that way. Thinking about it, you're absolutely right. It never occurred to me I was being so tactless when we met.'

'Oh, it's all right, forget it,' shrugged Jack.

'No, no. I've been thoughtless. How are you Jack?' Sam persisted.

'I'm fine.'

An awkward silence befell the two drinkers as neither knew what to say next. After a few moments, Sam put down his pint and turned to Jack.

'And how's your Bobby keeping?' he asked brightly.

9

Frank Haffey

I T was 15 April 1961, the year I joined Manchester United.
Being Irish I can be neutral when I say it was one of English
football's greatest days and one of Scotland's blackest. England
beat Scotland at Wembley by the incredible score of 9–3. I
wasn't there – I watched the highlights on television – but my
friend Denis Law was. He was playing for Scotland.

If you were English, it was a fabulous Saturday afternoon in
a sun-soaked Wembley stadium. If you were Scottish, it was
a nightmare. England sauntered, serenely confident, through
the first half reducing Scotland to a shambles. Four down
at half-time, the Scots came out fighting in the second half
and pulled back two goals. Denis tells me that even when
they were two goals adrift he didn't feel Scotland were out
of the hunt.

Then it happened: one of the most rip-roaring goal sprees
imaginable. England attacked the Scottish goal five times in the
space of ten minutes and scored five goals! There were five
principal executioners for England: Bryan Douglas of Blackburn
Rovers, Jimmy Greaves and Bobby Smith of Spurs, Fulham's
Johnny Haynes and Bobby Charlton of Manchester United.
Together they put Scotland to the sword and brought England's
goal tally to an incredible aggregate of thirty-two in their last
five international matches.

Apart from the scoreline, one of the most extraordinary

aspects of the game was the performance of the Scottish goalkeeper, Frank Haffey. Haffey played for Celtic and had been preferred over a much more accomplished goalkeeper, Bill Brown of Spurs. Poor Frank: it was a dog day. 'Frank started the game playing crap,' Denis told me, 'and got worse.'

It's a well-known fact that goalkeepers are a different breed. Like things that go bump in the night, they defy analysis. It's a truth universally acknowledged that a goalkeeper is one sandwich short of a picnic, that a player must be off his head to be one. Frank Haffey was no exception. As Denis tells me, what can be said about a goalkeeper who sings in the bath after letting in nine goals, most of which were his fault? The fact that Frank had a good voice was neither here nor there!

In those days, the England-Scotland game was played on a Saturday afternoon whilst a full programme of English and Scottish League fixtures took place at the same time. The game was not shown on television until later that night. Frank came out of the bath, dressed and made his way to the nearest telephone to ring his parents to let them know how he and Scotland had performed. He told them the game had been a twelve-goal thriller!

As if the Scottish players weren't feeling bad enough, during the buffet reception for players and officials, a lively Frank was buzzing around the room trying to find out if the nine goals were a record.

'Oh, it's not so bad,' he told his dejected and depressed Scottish team-mates. 'Remember, we lost a battle against the English at Culloden.'

'Aye,' Scottish wing half Dave Mackay said, 'But after Culloden we didn't have to put our suits on and have sandwiches with the bastards.'

When the Scottish players left Wembley the English press were clamouring for a photograph. 'I've got a great idea for your photograph, boys!' an enthused Frank told the salivating

English photographers. He had. The next day the Sunday papers carried a picture of a smiling Frank standing, hands raised, palms outwards goalkeeper-style. Behind him was Big Ben, with the hands of the Westminster clock showing a quarter past nine!

To say Frank got the cold shoulder when he returned to Scotland is an understatement. Within a month he had emigrated to Australia, though there are those north of the border still convinced that he was deported.

In 1993, I was in Sydney, Australia with Denis Law doing a month of soccer coaching. Denis and I were in the car park of the coaching school on the point of leaving one evening when a self-conscious voice said, 'Hello, Denis.' It was none other than Frank Haffey. We chatted for a few minutes. Frank told Denis and me that he had never seen Scotland since his departure after the Wembley debacle thirty-two years previously.

'Is it safe for me to go back now?' he asked.

'No, not yet,' said Denis in all seriousness. 'Give it a few more years.'

Frank nodded solemnly before saying goodbye and making his way back to his car. Halfway across the car park, he turned towards us. 'The ninth was offside, you know,' he called.

I have not seen or heard of Frank since.

10

The Professional's Lot

JIMMY MURPHY, who was assistant manager to Matt Busby at Manchester United, told me that in the early sixties he received a letter from the manager of Cromptons Recs, an amateur side who played in the Lancashire Combination Division 2.

The letter recommended that Jimmy take a look at their centre forward, who, by coincidence, turned out to be the manager's son-in-law. Thinking that there was always a chance a footballing gem may have slipped through the net operated by the United scouts, Jimmy went along to assess the boy's potential.

After ten minutes watching the game, Jimmy was about to leave the ground when he was cornered by the manager, surprised that he was leaving so early. He told the manager that he had seen enough of the boy to convince him he didn't have what it took to make the jump from the amateur game to the professional ranks.

'So what's the difference between an amateur player and a professional player?' asked the manager.

'A professional can play well even when he doesn't have to,' said Jimmy, 'whereas an amateur couldn't play well even if he wanted to.'

I suppose that is one reason why some people are paid for playing football and others play for enjoyment. Of course, there comes a point in every professional's career when he feels he is not being paid enough for his services and then he will go and see the manager about a rise. More often than not, when it comes to getting a rise in mid-contract, you stand more chance of being able to knit with sawdust.

Following our League Championship victory in 1965, we United players felt we were worth a good increase in basic pay. Surely Matt Busby would not deny us a rise? After all, we had just brought the First Division Championship trophy back to Old Trafford for the first time since 1957 and we were once more eligible for the European Cup,

The consensus of opinion in the changing room was that each member of the first-team squad should be entitled to an extra £15 per week, irrespective of whether he played in the first team or not. That agreed, all we had to decide was who would go and negotiate with Matt on our behalf. There was only one taker.

'I'm the only obvious candidate,' said Denis Law, full of fortitude.

No one objected, because, in truth, no one fancied trying to lay down terms to the boss. If Denis felt he could do it, we wouldn't stand in his way. Thus Denis became our chief negotiator.

'Don't let the boss talk you down to ten quid,' said Bobby Charlton.

'Aye, stick to your guns, Lawman,' Paddy Crerand added. 'We've just won the League, the ball is in our court. We want the full fifteen quid.'

Denis swaggered about the changing room and assured us all he had the measure of Matt Busby. 'Leave the boss to me,' he said boastfully. 'He may be a canny Scot where money is concerned, but so am I. You did the best thing letting me handle this for you. Mark my words, the boss doesn't intimidate me!'

Off he went for his appointment with Matt Busby and we all sat eagerly awaiting the outcome.

'We could be here for some time,' Nobby Stiles said. 'Once

Denis and the boss start arguing, it could be hours before the boss gives way.'

No sooner had Nobby spoken than the door of the dressing room opened and in walked Denis. He had been away only ten minutes at the most. 'Well?' we chorused.

'Bad news,' said Denis, scuffing his feet on the floor of the changing room. 'I told the boss I was negotiating on behalf of all of us. We argued for a few minutes. He pleaded poverty. In the end I was lucky to get out agreeing on five pounds.'

A chorus of disappointed sighs filled the room. 'It's nowhere near what we wanted.' said Paddy Crerand, miffed.

'No, but it's better than nothing,' I said.

Denis sheepishly gathered his belongings together in his sports bag and crept quietly out of the room.

A week later, we all discovered that our pay packets were short and complained to Matt Busby. 'Take it up with your appointed negotiator,' he told us in the dressing room, pointing to a forlorn Denis Law. 'When he came to me making money demands, I told him how tight money really is and persuaded him to accept a wage cut of five pounds a man to help the club out.'

Recently, during a visit to Glasgow, my old mate Jim Baxter told me of the high life he enjoyed in the late fifties and early sixties at his first club, Raith Rovers. Raith were managed by a wily old Scot called Bert Herdman. Whenever Raith played a home game or an away game within reasonable travelling distance of Kirkcaldy, the Fife home of the club, the team always enjoyed a post-match high tea in a local hotel. The routine was always the same. The Rovers players would arrive with Bert and sit down to egg or beans on toast, followed by tea and a selection of cakes.

In 1961, Raith were due to meet Glasgow Celtic at their home ground, Starks Park. Rovers were perilously near the foot of the table and relegation was staring them in the face. Desperate for the points that would keep them in the First Division, where the club would benefit from the big money-spinning games against the likes of Rangers, Celtic, Hearts and Aberdeen, Bert Herdman told the players they were on a big bonus if they beat Celtic. 'I've spoken to the directors,' he said, 'and they've assured me that if you win today, each and every one of you will receive the biggest bonus ever offered by the club.'

The team played out of their skins that day and beat Celtic 1–0. After the game the dressing room was jubilant. On the bus journey to the local hotel, the ecstatic players pressed Bert about their bonus. 'I'll tell you what it is when we get to the hotel,' he said.

On arriving at the hotel the players filed into the dining room and took their seats. Bert Herdman stood amongst them, hands behind his back. 'Well, ye did it today, all right, boys,' he said with pride. 'I promised ye a big bonus if ye beat Celtic, and ye did that right enough!'

The players shuffled in their seats with expectancy.

'So today,' Bert went on, pausing for effect before throwing his arms out wide like some preacher from the American mid-west, 'te hell with beans on toast. Let's go *à la carte*!'

I can recall situations where the boot was on the other foot when it came to negotiating wages and bonuses. In 1970, I went to see the then United manager, Wilf McGuinness, about a new contract. I had been United's leading goalscorer for the past four seasons. What was more, I had been the leading provider of goals for the likes of Denis Law and Brian Kidd the previous season. Along with Denis, I was the joint fourth leading scorer for United of all time with 128 League goals. Money-wise, I felt I was worth more than I was being offered. 'I want thirty thousand a year,' I told Wilf.

'Thirty thousand a year!' said Wilf, somewhat surprised. 'But that's more than the chairman of British Leyland got last year!'

'I know,' I said, 'but I had a better year.'

11

Baxter's Pink Form

Like me, Jim Baxter has fought a battle with the booze. I know he won't mind me saying it, but Jim went a lot further down that dark and dismal road than I did. A few days before Christmas 1992, he was rushed into hospital and we nearly lost dear Jim – on his own admission, he was at death's door. Fortunately for him and his good lady, Norma, Jim pulled himself back from the brink and now, thankfully, seems to have his drinking under control. I certainly hope so, because when I travel north of the border to Glasgow, I never tire of hearing Jim spinning tales of his playing days in Scotland with Raith Rovers and Glasgow Rangers.

Jim began his senior football career in the late fifties with Kirkcaldy-based Raith Rovers. He was signed by their manager, Bert Herdman, from a junior team called Crossgates Primrose. 'I was paid seven and six a week if I was chosen to play,' Jim told me, 'That's thirty-seven pence. And five shillings, the equivalent of twenty-five pence, if I didn't.'

The bonus system at this club was, as far as I know, unique. If a player played in the first team, in addition to receiving his money he got a hot meat pie.

'You may laugh, George. But the meat in those pies was really something else!' Jim told me, adding impishly, 'God knows what it was, but it wasn't meat, that's for sure.'

Jim was eighteen when he was invited to sign for Raith Rovers. He tells me he felt somewhat out of place when he turned up for his first day's training to find the next eldest to him was a player called Willie Bolland, nicknamed 'The Young Boy', who was twenty-six. It was a Dad's Army of a team. No one knew for sure how old the goalkeeper was, but the rumour in the dressing room was that his National Insurance number was 4. 'His forehead had so many wrinkles, he had to screw his cap on,' said Jim.

Also in that side was a centre forward called Ernie Copland who had played for Raith for longer than anyone could remember. Ernie had pipe-cleaner legs, was as bald as a billiard ball and, with the advent of every new season, took out a new life-insurance policy against collapsing and dying on the pitch. According to Jim, if Ernie had gone during a game, Prudential would have gone as well.

The Rovers manager, Bert Herdman, didn't know much about football, but he did know how to keep the club running on a shoestring. He had to wheel and deal as best he could, because the club couldn't afford to pay him or any of the players very much in the way of wages. When the hot water went off at one of the local collieries, Bert did a deal with the pit management, allowing the miners on early shift to use the plunge bath at the club to wash. When the Raith players used the same bathwater after training, the water was so black, the players were dirtier when they came out of the bath than they had been when they got in.

It was 1961 and Raith upset the applecart by going to Ibrox, the home of Rangers, and winning by 3–2. Jim turned in a brilliant performance at left half and dictated the game. 'Rangers were lucky to get away with conceding three that day,' he recalls. 'Their crossbar had a blinder. They had a goalkeeper called George Niven who was so bad, a clean sheet for him started at three goals.'

The Tuesday following the famous victory over Rangers, Jim was called into Bert Herdman's office. At the time, there were three types of players' registration forms in Scotland. A white

form, which was for amateur players, a green form for professionals and a pink form. The pink one, also for professionals, dictated that if the player was sold on to another club, both he and the person who had signed him originally would receive a percentage of the transfer fee.

Jim was only a young boy who wanted nothing more than to play football and cared nothing for paperwork and the like. 'I want you to sign this pink form, Jim, son,' Bert told him, pushing it across his desk.

'Aye, OK, Mr Herdman,' Jim said. 'What is it?'

'What is it?' Bert repeated incredulously. 'Why, son, it means money for you, more money than you've ever seen in your life and all you have to do to get it is sign this pink form!'

Jim's eyes lit up. 'Money for me? How much?' he asked, his body all a shake.

'Five pounds!' said Bert boastfully as he threw himself back in his chair.

Jim had never had as much as £5 in his life, so without hesitation, he put pen to paper. Bert produced a crisp, new, five-pound note from the drawer of his desk and handed it over to an elated Jim. As Jim left his manager's office, he thought he'd really landed on his feet. Five pounds for signing a form!

The next day, Jim was called once more into Bert's office. When he entered, Bert was not alone. A distinguished-looking man in his early fifties with thin, silver hair was sitting there. Jim was told to sit down and Bert introduced the man as Scot Symon, the manager of Glasgow Rangers.

'Mr Symon is here to sign you,' Bert told Jim. 'I've made all the arrangements. Don't ask about a signing-on fee. Don't ask about wages, they'll pay you well enough. Just accept what you're being offered. Say yes to everything Mr Symon says and sign this transfer form.'

Jim did as he was told and immediately joined the mighty Rangers.

Some months later, Jim found out that because he had signed the pink form, a percentage of the transfer fee had gone to Bert Herdman and himself. It amounted to £1,000. When Glasgow Rangers next visited Raith Rovers, Jim was determined to confront Bert about the issue of the money. 'You sly bastard!' he said, cornering Bert in the Rovers Social Club after the match. 'I made five pounds out of my transfer to Rangers and you made nine hundred and ninety-five quid!'

Bert put a fatherly arm around Jim, gazed off into the distance and smiled warmly as he swelled with pride. 'Aye, Jim, son,' he said, a lump in his throat. 'We both made a killing that day, right enough.'

12

Everything on the Line

I N the ten years spanning the mid-sixties to the mid-seventies, Glasgow Celtic reigned supreme. They won nine successive League Championships, the Scottish FA Cup seven times and the League Cup five times. They were, to my mind, one of the best-ever British club sides.

There are those who say too much success brings complacency. Not for the great Celtic team that Jock Stein put together. When it came to winning trophies, they were as hungry as the jaws of hell. To prove it, for all the domestic trophies they ran away with, Celtic also brought the European Cup to Glasgow. The legs of the table in the trophy room creaked and groaned like those of a seasoned old pro asked to take part in a charity game.

Today, Premier League managers and players complain of too many matches. Was it ever thus? In the season Celtic won the European Cup, they competed in sixty-seven games from pre-season to season's end. The players loved playing and when they weren't, they were as restless as the wind. Not once did you hear them protest at there being too many matches. There's a saying in football about injuries – 'Nothing hurts when you're winning' – which is also applicable to matches. When you're playing well, enjoying football and winning, there is no tiredness or fatigue and, above all, no complaints. That is why, when Jimmy Johnstone received a telephone call from the Scottish manager, Walter McCrae, saying he had been selected for the national team, he welcomed with open arms the chance to play football for his country.

Jimmy was the sort of player I loved to watch in action. Known as Jinky, he stood no more than 5 feet 5 inches tall and looked like the schoolboy whose resourceful mother had bought school clothes for him to grow into. The famous green and white hooped shirt was too large and hung on his body like a poncho, the sleeves like concertinas. The round collar of the shirt gave football it's first 'off the shoulder' look and a bullet head of ginger hair was cropped so short it made an American marine's crew-cut look positively hippy.

Yet for all his slight form, Jinky was a footballer of giant talent. His low centre of gravity and his mesmerising skills meant he was a full back's nightmare. He had a terrific turn of pace and many was the time his acceleration over ten yards was enough to leave a full back panting like a forge bellows in his wake.

Jinky received his first Scottish international call-up in 1965 for a game against Wales and was as happy as the birds in spring as he informed his team-mates of his selection in the Parkhead dressing room before training. The Scotland squad was to assemble at a hotel in Ayrshire and, to give an extra edge to Jinky's joy, were to play Celtic behind closed doors at Rugby Park, the home of Kilmarnock, on the Saturday preceding the Wednesday-night game.

This friendly was the cause of much good-humoured banter between those Celtic players selected for the Scottish squad and those who would have to turn out against them. Much pride was at stake and it was obvious that the so-called 'friendly practice match' would have a highly competitive edge to it as far as the 'bhoys' were concerned.

Come the day, Walter McCrae, who was then also manager of Kilmarnock, called his charges into the home-team dressing room at Rugby Park and announced the starting line-up for the game against Celtic. He then went on to name the substitutes.

Jinky felt like the symptoms on a medicine bottle. His name and that of Chris Shevlane from Hearts had not been mentioned.

Just as McCrae was about to round up his team talk, he turned to Jinky and Shevlane to tell them that they too had an important role to play that day. Jinky's face lit up. Of course, he was to be the ace up McCrae's sleeve; he would be introduced in the second half, a fresh pair of legs that would twist and turn on a sixpence and run his Celtic colleagues ragged.

'I've sorted out a referee for this afternoon,' said McCrae. 'But I want you two to be linesmen. Your kit is over there.' He pointed to two shiny black linesman's strips folded on the kit skip.

Jinky's face fell. Anger welled up inside him. It was bad enough to have the excitement of being called up for the national side tempered by the fact that he had been asked to be a linesman in a practice match; but against Celtic, of all teams. Back in the Parkhead dressing room following the game, his life would not be worth living. He would be ragged about it for months. His reputation on the line, literally, Jinky refused to don the linesman's garb. He stormed out of the dressing room and spent the entire game sitting as mute as Pygmalion, with only Chris Shevlane for company in the empty, cavernous grandstand of Rugby Park.

Two weeks later, Jinky was back at Rugby Park, this time for a League game between Walter McCrae's Kilmarnock and Celtic. At the time, Kilmarnock were a very useful outfit. They had clinched the Scottish League Championship in dramatic style on the last day of the 1964–65 season on goal average. The likes of Bobby Ferguson, Andy King, Frank Beattie and Tommy McLean were forces to be reckoned with and a recent 2–2 draw with Real Madrid in the European Cup showed they were not green around the gills when it came to European competition.

Kilmarnock were good, but on this day Celtic, and in particular Jinky Johnstone, put them to the sword.

Jinky was inquisitor and executioner as he at first tamed then tortured the team. The home side were never in it. Midway through the second half, Celtic were 5–0 to the good with Jinky, having scored two and made two, hungry for more.

Walter McCrae sat morosely in the dugout as genius flowed from Jinky's boots. With ten minutes remaining, Jinky latched on to a pass from Bobby Murdoch deep in his own half and took flight down the wing. It was as if the ball were glued to his boot. He evaded one tackle then another before cutting inside. Here his pace saw off two blue and white striped shirts before he veered back out to the wing once more. He beat Jim McFadzean, the Kilmarnock left back, then turned back and beat him again. Foot on the ball, Jinky waited for his full back to recover. Then, with a shimmy and a flick of his hips, he sent McFadzean one way and the crowd the other before darting into the penalty box and hitting a swerving shot past the flaying arms of Bobby Ferguson into the far corner of the net for his hat-trick.

Jinky accepted the congratulations of his team-mates and trotted back to take his place out wide on the halfway line for the restart. As he did so, he turned and caught sight of Walter McCrae in the dugout. McCrae's head was bowed, his face contorted as he wearily rubbed the corners of his eyes with a thumb and forefinger. Suddenly, McCrae looked up and his eyes focused on Jinky, standing only three feet away on the touchline.

'Not bad for a bloody linesman, eh, Walter?' he said, flicking his head to one side and grinning impishly.

13

Avi Cohen

I T is always pleasing to get invitations to attend games from friends in football. In the main, of course, these invitations emanate from Manchester United or clubs who are playing United and think I would like to see the game as their guest.

During the 1980–81 season I went to a Boxing Day match at Anfield between Liverpool and United as the guest of the then Liverpool chairman, John Smith. A huge crowd of over 51,000 turned up to see Liverpool run out 2–0 winners with goals from Alan Hansen and David Johnson. After the game, I was renewing old acquaintances, chatting with Kenny Dalglish, Terry McDermott and Ray Kennedy, when I was introduced to the Liverpool full back Avi Cohen.

Avi had joined Liverpool from the Israeli side Maccabi Tel Aviv and, although a very accomplished player, had found it difficult to break into the Liverpool first team. The previous season, Avi had made four first-team appearances, one as a substitute, when Liverpool won the First Division Championship using just seventeen players throughout the season. He had found it difficult to dislodge Phil Neal or Alan Kennedy from either of the full back positions, but I told him he had done well to break into the first team at all considering the number of quality players who were competing for the full back position.

Even the competition for a place at full back in the reserve team at Anfield was tough at that time. Avi was in contention with

Brian Kettle, who is now manager of Southport; Colin Irwin; Alan Harper, who would go on to win First Division Championship and FA Cup-winners' medals with Everton, before playing for Manchester City, Sheffield Wednesday and Luton Town; Dave Watson, who was to leave Anfield and try his luck with Norwich City before returning to Merseyside and joining Everton; Richard Money, who would break into the Anfield first team before moving to Luton; and Alex Cribley, who later joined Aston Villa. Looking back, that list reminds you of just what strength in depth the Liverpool squad had at that time – and this was only the defence!

I chatted for a time with Avi and asked him how he was adjusting to life on Merseyside.

'It must have been quite a culture shock, stepping on to a plane in Tel Aviv and hours later being driven through the streets of Liverpool, knowing this was your new home,' I said. Avi agreed that it was and went on to tell me about the problems he had had explaining his change of lifestyle to his mother when he telephoned home to Tel Aviv.

'Do you still wear your skull cap?' asked his mother.

'No one wears skull caps in Liverpool,' Avi explained.

'I hope you still go to the synagogue every morning.'

'That's impossible now,' Avi said. 'We train every morning. It's my job, there's no time for daily synagogue.'

'Well, at least you still go on the Sabbath.' said his mother.

'No,' Said Avi. 'How can I? Over here they play their football on Saturdays.'

'Tell me you managed to attend synagogue on Yom Kippur, at least?' his mother asked, exasperated.

'I couldn't. We were playing Dinamo Tbilisi in the European Cup, I was one of the substitutes and had to travel with the team.'

He then told his mother that he must be going because he had to join the rest of the Liverpool players. They were leaving by coach for the Moat House Hotel for the club's Christmas party.

'Oy vey! You're celebrating Christmas now?' his mother asked, deeply shocked.

'All the players are going. It would be unsociable of me not to go.' Avi reasoned. 'This is Liverpool. The way of life is different here. It's not Tel Aviv.'

There were a few seconds of silence as Avi waited for his mother to continue the strained conversation.

'You can say that again!' his despondent mother said finally. 'Tell me, are you still circumcised?'

Life at United

'I gave up trying to go home at five-thirty years ago. The draw of this club is too strong.'

Sir Matt Busby

'Matt always believed Manchester United would be one of the greatest clubs in the world.
'He was the eternal optimist – in 1968 he still hoped Glenn Miller was just missing.'

Paddy Crerand

14

The Competitive Spirit

Back home in Belfast, my dad, like parents the world over, keeps an album of his children. He and my mum had started it when they first had a family and amongst the photographs are several taken of me when I was a toddler. In one, I'm seen playing outside Granny Withers' house in Donald Street at the tender age of fourteen months. Most friends, on seeing them, say something along the lines of, 'You can see he'd got football in him even then, can't you?' or, 'You can see the competitive spirit even then, George.'

Well, I don't think Sir Matt Busby would have jumped at the chance of signing me then, but the competitive spirit I am supposed to have shown has stayed with me throughout my life. It's particularly important in football, of course. Without it there would be no contest.

One of the aspects of my game that used to please Sir Matt was the fact that if I lost the ball I would immediately give chase and fight to get it back. Many people forget nowadays that one of the strongest parts of my game was actually my tackling. I used to think it was a personal insult if a member off the opposition took the ball off me. The competitive spirit would fire me to get it back. It's a spirit I see in Ryan Giggs; if he loses the ball he never seems satisfied until he has won it back and it's at his feet again.

Both Denis Law and Nobby Stiles had that spirit aplenty. It coursed through their veins and showed itself in everything they did, whether it was playing in a game, training or even entertaining the team in a hotel as we prepared for an away match.

The 1967–68 season was a vintage one. The year before we had won the League Championship and the season would culminate in us lifting the European Cup. These were heady days indeed, and the 'House Full' signs at Old Trafford were getting weather beaten. Such was the club's ambition to follow the Championship by winning the European title, it was decided that nothing would side-track or detract us. That season, Manchester United were the only team not to take part in the League Cup!

We had travelled to Ipswich for a League game and arrived at our hotel on the Friday at around 5.30 p.m. Like most players, I always found the stay in a hotel before a game about as exciting as watching a tortoise on a lettuce hunt. You can't truly relax because of the game the following day. You're not allowed a drink and the evening is usually whiled away playing cards and snooker or reading a book.

After the evening meal, the players were left to entertain themselves until bedtime around ten o'clock. We had assembled in the hotel lounge when a disgruntled Denis Law appeared to inform us that the hotel did not have a games room of any description. With no prospect of snooker, I was on the point of returning to my room with a book when Denis suggested we play some games to test our competitive spirit.

He gathered everyone around. It was decided we'd all put ten bob in a kitty and whoever told the biggest lie would win the money.

Now, as great a guy as Denis is, no one was prepared to let him judge who was the best liar. After much debate it was decided that Bobby Charlton and I would sit the game out and act as judges. The players would be paired off against one another and the competition would be run on a knock-out basis until we had two finalists.

One by one the pairs would come before Bobby and me and we

72

would listen to their lie, confer and decide whose was the biggest. Eventually we had two finalists, Denis and Nobby Stiles. As the competition progressed, the lies told had become more and more outrageous and the laughter from everyone got louder and louder. In the final, our sergeant-at-arms, Paddy Crerand, brought Nobby and Denis before us. I indicated that Nobby should go first.

'Remember two years ago when we went on that pre-season tour of Canada and the USA?' Nobby asked as he went for the prize of the kitty. 'When we stayed in a hotel that overlooked the head of Niagara Falls?'

Bobby and I nodded.

'Well, one morning I got up early. Whilst you lot were all in bed, I took my trunks and towel and went down to the lake at the foot of the falls; swam across the lake, then, just because I couldn't be bothered to walk the long route back up to the hotel, I swam up Niagara Falls. All the way to the top.'

The rest of the players cheered, whistled and clapped their hands in approval of Nobby's inventiveness. Once Bobby and I had restored order, we indicated that it it was Denis's turn.

'I was there when he did it!' Denis said, leaning over to pick up the kitty.

15

Handling Players

MATT BUSBY was a master tactician not only on the field, but off it as well. He had a very laid-back way of getting things done, but get them done he did, and what's more, they were done his way. Whether he was giving the team a pep talk prior to an important game or telling the players which rooms they had been allocated in a hotel, his voice was always relaxed and soothing. In many ways it was hypnotic – he had the ability to make even the most mundane tasks sound wonderful. As Wilf McGuinness, the first-team coach used to say, if Matt told you to go to hell, you'd actually look forward to the trip.

To call Matt 'a canny Scot' would be doing him an injustice. He was clever, possessed a firm understanding of people's behaviour and took the time to get to know the idiosyncrasies of his players. If our centre half, Bill Foulkes, was not performing to his potential, Matt knew a gentle reminder, rather than a lambasting, would make him raise his game.

After an FA Cup tie at home to Sunderland in 1964, in which we conceded three goals and were lucky to get a draw, Matt took Bill back out on to the pitch. They stood outside the tunnel by the touchline and for a minute or so Matt said nothing.

'Where is it, Bill?' he asked eventually, his eyes scanning the penalty area across to his right.

'Where's what, boss?' Bill said nervously.

'The hole in the pitch,' said Matt calmly.

Bill shuffled his feet uneasily, not knowing what Matt was taking about.

'What hole, boss?' he asked.

'The bloody hole you hid in for half an hour whilst three goals were put up us!'

Each manager has his own way of addressing problems and dealing with players who do not perform well. I always feel a manager must know the emotional and psychological make-up of his players as best he can in order to get the most from them. Some respond to a right rollicking; some don't and will withdraw into a shell.

In 1973–74, having just escaped relegation the previous season, Manchester United were relegated to Division 2. As the season drew to a close, United were scrapping for points and were beaten 1–0 in an away game at Everton. The jaws of relegation yet again opened wide.

This was a United with Tommy Docherty as manager. And United without me – I had walked out in January after playing only twelve games that season – without Denis Law, who had gone to Manchester City, and without Bobby Charlton, who had retired. At half-time at Goodison Park, Tommy Docherty was not pleased with the performances of one or two players, in particular, full back Stewart Houston.

'You effing useless toe-rag! the Doc bellowed at Stewart.' Call yourself a full back? You've been absolute shit out there. Hear me, son? You've been rubbish. A pile of crap! In fact the biggest load of crap I have ever seen pull on a football shirt. Crap! Crap!! Crap!!! That's you, son!' Stewart Houston sat and stared down at his boots, taking it all.

'An absolute disgrace, that's what you are!' the Doc screamed on. 'A dis-frigging-grace to that red shirt you're wearing. In that first half, you were S. H. I. T. And that spells shit, son!'

The Doc paused for breath and for a moment an uneasy silence descended. It was broken by midfield player Lou Macari. 'Don't

beat about the bush, boss,' said Lou, his voice heavy with sarcasm. 'Tell the lad how he's really been playing!'

At Old Trafford, as you leave the home-team dressing room and walk down the corridor towards the tunnel that leads to the pitch, you pass the referee's changing room. It's not a large room, only some 12 feet by 12 feet, but the referee shares it with his two linesmen.

On a Friday morning, we would do some light training at Old Trafford before collecting our wages and finishing for the day at around noon. Matt would sit in the referee's room as we made our way down the corridor to the pitch. The trick was to get past the room without being called into it. If you heard your name called, it was almost certain you were going to be left out of the first team the next day.

In 1963, Nobby Stiles was in and out of the team. Just when he thought he had secured a regular place, he'd be left out. Nobby was always told of his fate on a Friday morning, in the referee's room. It got to the stage where Nobby dreaded walking down the corridor and passing the infamous room. He'd tiptoe past, only to be summoned by Matt.

'Nobby? Have you got a minute?'

The door was always open and Matt would sit to the right of the room, leaning forward, hands clasped together. 'How do you think you've been playing?' Matt would ask Nobby.

'OK, boss. Think I've been playing all right.' Nobby would say nervously.

'You're out tomorrow,' Matt would say, matter-of-factly, before telling Nobby the arrangements for the reserve team game taking place the following day.

It happened so often that Nobby started to get a complex about it. 'Do what I do,' fellow midfield player, Johnny Giles, told him one Friday morning. 'If the boss calls you in today and asks how you think you are playing, tell him you're playing well,' he said

with an air of superiority. 'Say to the boss, "Didn't you see me against the opposition's inside forward last Saturday? I never gave him a kick." Be positive and confident, convince him he can't do without you.'

Nobby listened intently and was visibly more confident when he left the dressing room and headed towards the pitch.

'Nobby? Have you got a minute?' Matt's voice called from within the ref's room.

Nobby went in, feeling very positive as he presented himself.

'How do you think you've been playing?' Matt asked.

'Very well!' said Nobby cheerfully. 'Didn't you see me against that Everton inside forward last Saturday? I never gave him a kick. I played well. In fact, the way I'm playing, you can't do without me, boss!'

'But do you think you can play better than you have been?' asked Matt.

'Yes,' replied Nobby without thinking.

'You're out tomorrow.'

16

Murphy's Law

EVEN though we were the League Champions in 1967, training at the Manchester United training ground, the Cliff, under assistant manager Jimmy Murphy did not afford us the quality of life enjoyed by the Premier League players of today. In terms of the luxuries and designer kits that are accepted as part and parcel of training by today's star players, United's teams had more than a little in common with those who enjoy their game in the local Sunday-morning Leagues.

Before training began, the players assembled in the tiny dressing room that boasted a single window. This was rectangular, long and, because of the wire reinforcement within the pitted glass itself, offered about as much light as a fairylight bulb. Each player had his own spot in the dressing room. As soon as he entered, he would head for 'his' place and sit down. When a new signing arrived, he'd wait around until everyone was seated then claim the one vacant seat left by the outgoing player he had replaced.

Jimmy Murphy would enter with a large, grey sack and tip it out on to the floor. The players would jump from their seats and dive towards the tumbling kit, frantically searching for the few good pairs of socks. However, this was all beneath Shay Brennan, who let everyone squabble over the kit. He'd wait until we were all kitted out and take what socks remained. This was the reason why Shay Brennan was always seen training in a) odd socks, b) socks with holes in them, or c) odd socks with holes in them.

And so would begin a United training session, with the following scenario taking place almost daily . . .

'This shirt's still damp from when it was washed!' Tony Dunne complains to Jimmy Murphy.

'It won't do you any harm,' Murphy tells him. 'It'll dry out quickly once you start running about outside.'

Tony Dunne reluctantly puts on a pair of damp socks as well, worrying that he'll end up with rheumatism when he's older. Murphy reminds everyone not to leave any valuables behind in the dressing room – there will be no one left at the Cliff to safeguard the premises when we go on the warm-up run. He nods towards young Brian Kidd, who produces from his kitbag a string-drawn soap bag and proceeds to go around the room, asking each player in turn, 'Any valuables?'

Each player tells Kiddo what he is dropping into his bag in case there is a discrepancy later. How Kiddo is expected to remember who has given him what, no one knows. Eventually he hands Murphy the soap bag bulging with money, watches, keys and rings. Jimmy Murphy secretes it away at the bottom of his medical box.

Bill Foulkes, the largest man in the dressing room, struggles to get into a pair of size 34 shorts. He looks ridiculous and complains to Murphy. 'There's a pair of forty-two's around here somewhere,' Murphy tells him.

No one owns up to having a pair of size 42 shorts. Eventually, Murphy notices that Nobby Stiles, the smallest man in the room, is wearing a huge pair. Nobby refuses to swap and a good-natured argument begins. Eventually Murphy intervenes, lays down the law and Nobby reluctantly agrees to swap shorts with Bill Foulkes.

'Count yourself lucky,' Denis Law tells Nobby. 'I thought I'd picked a good pair of shorts and ended up with these!' Denis displays the inside of his legs and reveals testicled underpants protruding through shorts ripped at the crotch.

'Kit doesn't last five minutes nowadays. They just don't make it to last,' says Bobby Charlton. Everyone agrees. 'Take these socks,' Bobby continues, holding up a pair. 'You take one kick on the leg and the socks have had it.'

'It's terrible when you think how much it all costs these days,' says Paddy Crerand.

I am stripped and ready first. 'What are we doing today, Jimmy?' I ask Murphy.

His answer is always the same. 'You'll find out soon enough.'

'Can we have five a side?'

'Five a side!' Murphy echoes with great sarcasm. 'Is that all you ever want to do, George? We're here to train, not play five a side all day.'

'Well, can we?' I ask, not having had an answer to my question.

'We'll see,' says Murphy.

The player who has been hogging the one and only loo for ten minutes emerges. Within seconds, those players changing nearest to the loo cry out in horror.

'What's up?' asks Alex Stepney from the far end of the room.

'You'll find out soon enough,' says Denis, coughing and spluttering.

'Bloody hell!' Stepney shouts as he and those near him waft hands in front of contorted faces.

'You ought to see a doctor,' says Tony Dunne, turning to the guilty party.

'It's not a doctor he needs,' says Denis. 'It's bloody Dynorod.'

Jimmy Murphy re-enters the room and tells the players to assemble outside. He takes some rubber traffic cones out on to the practice pitch. When he returns to the changing room, only Paddy Crerand remains. 'Hurry it up, Paddy. We're starting in a minute,' Murphy urges.

For the first time that morning, and only because Murphy is

standing over him, Paddy puts some urgency into his preparations. As he starts to lace his second boot, the lace snaps in two.

'Shit!'

'Tie it in a knot. It'll do for now,' Murphy advises tetchily and leaves the room shaking his head.

We are all sent on a warm-up run. John Aston, David Sadler and I are the first three players to complete it. In fact, we are the first three players back on every run we have ever been on. Likewise, Denis Law, Bill Foulkes and Paddy Crerand, the last three back, are always the last to return. Then come warm-up exercises, followed by shuttle runs and more strenuous exercises.

We lie prostrate on the ground and, as we carry out the exercises, Murphy walks amongst us, offering words of encouragement. 'And when I've got my back to you, no cheating!' he warns. 'Because you will only be cheating yourself.' We lie flat on our backs and are asked to raise our legs six inches off the ground, then open them wide apart. Close them. Open them again. This lasts for two minutes or so and produces more grunts and groans the longer it goes on.

'Now keep those legs raised until I count to ten,' Murphy orders.

His count reaches nine. 'Nine and a half,' he says with a grin. 'Nine and three quarters . . . Keep them raised!'

We grit our teeth and some question Murphy's parenthood.

There are screams of pain.

'Ten!'

Then a spontaneous exhalation of breath and sighs of relief as we all let leaded legs fall to the ground.

More loosening exercises, then across to the practice pitch. Murphy divides the players into two teams. To discriminate between the two sides, he asks one set of players to dispense with their shirts and play 'in skins'. The side chosen point out they were also 'skins' yesterday. Their protests fall on deaf ears.

The pitch is as hard as concrete, bumpy and rutted. 'If this was winter and the pitch was frozen this hard, we wouldn't be playing on it!' says Denis.

The ball seems full of air, difficult to control and always around knee height. Bobby tries one of his thunderbolts and the ball goes wide and is lost in a dense, nettle-filled undergrowth beyond the goal. It's a notorious place for lost balls. 'Don't take your eyes from the spot where the ball entered the undergrowth.' Murphy shouts.

Johnny Aston pulls his socks as far above his knees as possible before gingerly picking his way through the nettles to retrieve the ball. He pulls the cuffs of his shirt over each hand as he scoops up the ball and returns it to play.

At the side of the Cliff training ground there is a small car park with concrete posts dotted around it. Murphy has split everyone up into two groups. One group will play five a side on this tarmac square.

'These will help you be aware of what is around you!' Murphy points to the concrete posts on the small car park.

The tarmac square also has nuggets of broken glass scattered around it. Nobody is in the least concerned. Murphy drops the ball near Bobby Charlton and a fortune's worth of talent immediately springs into a five-a-side game on the dicey car park.

I am with the other group and we are taken into a small gymnasium which today is the players' lounge. We are told to get down on the floor and prop ourselves up by our hands and feet, facing upwards.

'Crab football. Off you go!' Murphy announces as he throws a ball in amongst us.

Everyone waddles in an ungainly manner across the floor. Denis has the ball and Tony Dunne, shoulderblades jerking violently, sets off in comic pursuit.

When training is over we return to the small changing room. As we throw our kit to the floor, Murphy implores us to 'put shorts and socks around the right way' to make life easier when it comes to collecting kit for the launderette. In the shower, Johnny Aston rinses the soap off his hair. As he bends down to rinse off any last suds, Nobby Stiles squirts a great dollop of shampoo on to the top of his head. He leaves the shower and enters the changing room, vigorously rubbing his hair with a towel.

Showers are at a premium at the Cliff. I share one with Shay Brennan. Denis arrives and wants to share it as well. We protest that there is no room for three. 'Then just let me wet my hair,' Denis says.

Shay and I stand slightly to one side to allow Denis to soak his hair. 'See, there is room for me,' Denis says, and proceeds to hog the shower.

Johnny Aston returns, fuming. 'Which bloody joker did this?' he demands to know, pointing to the frothing soapsuds in his hair.

Showers over, some players stand on spare towels, some on the bench seats as they dry themselves. Great billows of steam continue to waft into the dressing room from the shower. On a warm day it turns the room into a sauna.

'You can't get dry in this weather,' says Bobby after about ten minutes of rubbing himself down with a towel to no avail.

'Got the valuables?' Alex Stepney asks Murphy.

Murphy digs deep to the bottom of his medical box and produces Kiddo's string-drawn soap bag. One by one, the players collect their possessions as they trickle out of the dressing room and head for home.

I'm left there with Jimmy Murphy, who is standing there holding out a watch. 'Don't forget your watch, George.' I tell him it isn't mine.

Murphy stands amongst the debris of soiled and soaking kit, crumpled towels, tie-ups, used elastoplasts, discarded plastic cups and chewing-gum wrappers. A solitary tie is left hanging from one of the pegs. He goes into the shower area. I can hear him tutting to himself as he turns off a shower that has been left running, the cause of the continuous flow of steam into the dressing room.

As I leave, Murphy returns to the dressing room and looks at the watch in his hand. 'Bloody gold as well, look you,' he says. 'Trouble is, everything comes too easy for you players nowadays. You don't respect things.'

I say cheerio to him.

'Always the bloody same,' I hear him chunter to himself as I walk off. 'Somebody will always leave something.'

17

A Flying Winger

As someone who has flown all around the world, flying has never really bothered me. Only once in my life has air travel terrified me. It was at the beginning of the 1967–68 season in which United won the European Cup. Following our Championship win, I spent part of the 1967 summer break on holiday in Los Angeles. It was whilst travelling back to England to join United for pre-season training that I had one of the most traumatic moments of my life.

The stewardesses had just finished serving dinner on the plane when there was a terrific bang. Such was the noise, it was as if someone had hit the side of the plane in a car. I was just about to express my concern to the man next to me when suddenly the plane dropped like a stone.

People started to scream, the plane itself tilted forward at a violent angle and trays of food were sent careering down the aisle. My tray and food hit the floor and my neighbour's meal spilled all over my trousers. It was the least of my worries.

As the plane continued to plummet, people started to shout in fear and panic. I knew it was bad when I saw the stewardesses clinging to their seats and screaming. The man next to me grabbed my arm and held on to me – what he thought I could do I don't know.

Suddenly, the plane righted itself and the calming voice of the captain came through the speaker. To this day I can remember his words. 'Nothing to worry about, ladies and gentlemen. We hit some turbulence, then an air pocket. We've lost altitude, but we'll regain it soon enough. Please relax and continue to enjoy your meal.'

I would have continued the meal, if I could have found it amongst all the others scattered about the floor. I removed the arms of the man next to me from around my neck and joined the queue for the toilet. It was brown-trouser alert for everyone.

I can make light of the incident now, but at the time it was terrifying and, like many others on that plane, I prayed for the moment we landed safely at Heathrow. The incident made me very wary about flying again. With United participating in the European Cup I didn't want my anxiety to turn into a fear of flying and I thought I had succeeded in keeping a sense of proportion about it all.

When the first round of the European Cup was announced, we were drawn at home to the Maltese side Hibernians Valletta. I wasn't worried about the return leg until Paddy Crerand started recounting tales of how notorious the landings were in Malta. Paddy delighted in telling me that the airport runway had a terrible reputation; that even the airline captains were filled with fear at the mention of landing there. By the time Paddy had finished with me, the very thought of a flight to Malta scared me stiff.

The day before the game, I went in to see the boss, Matt Busby, and told him I didn't want to play in the second leg because I was worried about the flight. To my surprise, he was totally relaxed about it and told me I didn't have to play in the return match. There would be no need for me to go, he told me, if I turned it on in the first leg and we scored enough to give us a comfortable cushion for the away leg.

That night against Hibernians Valletta, I pulled every trick I knew. I felt as if I had covered every blade of grass on the Old Trafford pitch, being involved in every attack and defence when the opposition broke away. We ran out 4–0 winners and, as I left the pitch, the Valletta players formed a semi-circle and applauded me as I made my way up the tunnel.

Denis Law and David Sadler were congratulating me on my performance when Matt Busby entered the dressing room. The boss went around to every player, offering his own congratulations. Eventually he came to me. 'Well done, George, son. What a terrific game, out of the top drawer.' I felt as if a saint were speaking to me.

'Are you sticking to what you said about the away leg, boss?' I asked quietly.

Matt leaned towards me. 'Oh aye, George. You don't have to go.'

I was so relieved about not having to go through the ordeal of landing at Valletta that I almost jumped for joy.

After the game, there was a buffet reception for the players and officials of both sides. These normally passed off without any pomp or circumstance, but on this particular night, and unusually for him, Matt Busby wanted to say a few words. He stood up and welcomed our Maltese guests, adding that although they had lost 4–0 they had played sportingly and had never once resorted to unsavoury tactics.

As he finished, he beckoned the Valletta manager to come up and say a few words. The manager came to his side and Matt nodded to indicate that the visiting manager should speak.

'Lady and gen'men,' he said slowly and deliberately, his face showing great concentration. 'Please ... please ... you I beg ... do ... not ... deny ... the people of Malta ... the – how you say? – chance ... to see Georgie Best play.'

My chin must have dropped like Harrod's lift. The room broke into spontaneous applause as all seemingly agreed with his sentiment.

On the Friday following that Wednesday-night game, Matt

called me to his office. 'What can I do, George?' he asked me, arms outstretched.

'I know I said you didn't have to play in the return leg, but after their manager stood up and said what he said . . . well, the chairman Louis Edwards and the rest of the board are determined not to disappoint the Maltese people. They're insisting you go and they do, after all, pay our wages.'

I didn't want to go to Malta, but I understood Matt Busby's predicament. He was answerable to the board and I knew, if it was up to him alone, that he'd have kept his word and I'd be staying at home for the return leg. I had no choice.

On the day, Paddy Crerand and Denis Law did their best to allay my fears of flying by giving me regular dollops of whisky from a hip flask. Perhaps it was the drink, but the landing in Valletta was so smooth I hardly noticed it. I was left to wonder what I had been making such a fuss about.

The second leg wasn't up to much by way of a football match. The pitch had little in the way of grass, was as hard as a rock and bumpy. I trawled up and down the right flank with two or three Valletta players shadowing me. I couldn't create much, but by the same token, because they were giving me so much attention, neither could Valletta. We drew 0–0.

At the post-match reception, I was queuing along with players and club officials as we helped ourselves to a buffet laid out along one long table. I found myself next to someone I assumed was a Valletta club official, since he was wearing a club blazer and tie.

I asked him how long he had been with Hibernians Valletta and was surprised to hear him say that he wasn't a club official as such, but a lecturer from the local university.

'A university lecturer?' I enquired. 'So what are you doing here?'

The man went on to explain in impeccable English that he was a lecturer in languages, fluent in no fewer than five, and that the club employed him when they played in Europe to act as a translator. Valletta had hired him for the game against us because no one at the club could speak any English.

This perplexed me. 'But what about the manager?' I asked. 'He can speak English.'

'No, he only speaks Maltese.'

'But what about after the first leg in Manchester?' I said, somewhat confused. 'Your manager stood up and said those things about me.'

The lecturer thought for a moment as he recalled the incident. 'Ah, that little speech, yes,' he remembered eventually. 'Your manager, Mr Busby, because he had said a few words, insisted that our manager should say something too, in English. Our manager agreed, but because he does not know any English, Mr Busby taught him the sentence about you parrot fashion. He had no idea what it meant.'

Call it psychology if you like, but Matt cured me of any fears about flying.

18

A Team Talk

I N 1965, Manchester United reached the semi-final of the FA
Cup and were drawn against Leeds United. We drew the first
game 0–0 and eventually missed out on Wembley, losing the
replay 1–0. At the time, Leeds United had a reputation as the
dirtiest team in Britain and those who can remember playing
against them or watching them from the terraces will, I am sure,
agree that the reputation was entirely justified.

Matt Busby had Manchester United in his heart. He loved
the club and, in many respects, he was the driving force behind
making United the sort of club it is today. Nevertheless, he was
also a Scot, and fervently patriotic with it. This would come
to the fore in subtle ways, often in situations where you least
expected it. One such occasion was his team talk before that first
Cup semi-final against Leeds in 1965.

Assistant manager Jimmy Murphy had handed Matt the Leeds
United team sheet and Matt went through each member of
the side that day as he gave his team talk. 'Gary Sprake, the
goalkeeper,' he began. 'On his day, a nasty piece of work. Don't
let it be his day. Right back, Paul Reaney, dirty bastard. Left back,
Terry Cooper, even dirtier bastard. Right half, Johnny Giles, dirty
little bastard. Centre half, Jack Charlton. Dirty big bastard. Left
half, wee Billy Bremner . . .' Matt paused to ponder the Scottish
international midfield player who was one of the hardest players
in the Leeds team.

'. . . Bremner,' he continued. 'Good Scottish boy.'

19

Driving Ambition

Forwards receive the glory, midfield players the recognition, goalkeepers the admiration. Central defenders earn everyone's respect, but very rarely do the full backs merit any attention at all.

This is as true today as it was when Manchester United won the League Championship in 1967 and followed it the next season by winning the European Cup. Our two full backs were Shay Brennan and Tony Dunne, and if there were ever two unsung heroes of that side, it was those two. They were never outstanding or glittering in their performances in the way Denis Law or Bobby Charlton often were. Brennan and Dunne were dependable full backs who were in the side because they were consistent. During the seasons spannning 1965 to 1969, I could count on the fingers of one hand the number of bad games either of them had. When it came to a rock-steady performance on the field, as the boss Matt Busby used to say, Shay and Tony were as regular as an army drum.

The fact that both he and Tony were overlooked when the plaudits were being issued did occasionally rankle with Shay Brennan. Ninety-nine per cent of the time he would be his normal self, a warm, laid back Irishman with a wry wit. On the odd occasion, however, he would take issue about his anonymity and put forward a case for recognition for what he and Tony had contributed to a game.

It was the 1968–69 season and we had thrashed Queen's Park Rangers 8–1 at home on the Saturday. I sat with the rest of the players in the dressing room of our training ground, the Cliff, reading the reports of the game in the Monday newspapers. Suddenly, Shay Brennan threw down a couple of papers in disgust. He had read every match report and was, he complained, the only player not to be mentioned.

Most of us agreed that it was an injustice, but Shay was having none of our sympathy. When assistant manager Jimmy Murphy arrived, Shay directed his moans and grief towards him. Jimmy told him not to take any notice of what the newspapers said about a game and that all that mattered was what he and the boss thought of Shay's performances. As far as they were concerned, Jimmy said, Shay had an excellent game.

Normally Shay would have left it at that, but on this particular morning, he really had a bee in his bonnet about it. Whether it was because we had had such a resounding victory on the Saturday I don't know, but Shay wouldn't let Jimmy off the hook. On and on he went, until Shay was not only saying he received no recognition for what he contributed, but also that a full back's job was one of the most difficult on the field.

Jimmy Murphy indulged in some gentle mickey-taking at Shay's expense in response to this. It was like pouring petrol on hot coals. Within minutes Shay was tackling Jimmy Murphy about his job as assistant manager and claiming that he could do it better than Jimmy.

Jimmy used to visit a number of colleges, such as teacher training colleges, where he would give a short demonstration of coaching techniques to would-be PE teachers, then answer any questions the students might have about teaching football skills or football in general. Shay began to tease Jimmy about these visits. Jimmy could never have played full back in his playing days, he said, whereas he could not only easily do the job of assistant manager, he could take those lectures in his stride as well.

The conversation between the two started to get quite heated, so I suggested that Shay should be allowed to prove his point by taking Jimmy's place for the next coaching lecture.

Denis Law wondered how Jimmy and the rest of us would know what sort of job Shay had made of the coaching demonstration and lecture. After much discussion, it was decided that Shay would pretend to be Jimmy, and Jimmy would go along as well, pretending to be his driver. This was quite feasible, for although many people had heard of Jimmy Murphy, many would not recognise him if he passed them on the street.

The next session and lecture was due to take place the following week at a teacher training establishment called Alsager College, not far from Crewe in south Cheshire. As the date approached, I thought Shay might drop out and that would be an end to the matter. No, come the day, Shay was keener than ever to prove his point.

The pair duly arrived at Alsager College, where Shay introduced himself to the PE lecturers as Jimmy Murphy, assistant manager of Manchester United, and Jimmy as his chauffeur.

All went well during the practical demonstration of coaching out on the pitch with the students. In the lecture hall, Shay stood up and gave a passable performance talking about coaching. He seemed to be proving his point. After about ten minutes or so, the head of the PE department stood up and invited his students to ask questions. Again, Shay coped adequately until the fourth question came from the floor.

'In addition to being assistant manager of Manchester United, Mr Murphy, you are also manager of Wales. How would you incorporate the coaching ideas you've shown us today so that they would be effective in your forthcoming international against Brazil?'

Shay felt his mouth go dry. The room was silent. He cleared his throat and leaned on the rostrum in front of him. 'If you don't mind me saying so, this is a very naive question.' he said. 'In fact, the answer to it is simple. Very simple indeed.' He rubbed sweaty palms on the front of his jacket before continuing. 'In fact the answer is so simple, I'm going to ask my chauffeur at the back of this hall to answer it for you.'

20

Voice From the Crowd

A lot of players don't like Christmas games. A Boxing Day match means you can't indulge yourself with food, drink and celebration. More often than not, players spend most of Christmas Day away from their families in the team hotel. However, I always liked them.

It probably goes back to my childhood. Like all children, Christmas with my mum and dad was something I looked forward to for weeks on end. My dad was, and still is, a football fanatic. Nothing could equal the excitement I felt on Christmas morning when I peered into the pillowcase that was left at the end of my bed to find a new pair of football boots. Further down, I would also discover those two mainstays of all football-mad boys at that time, *Charles Buchan's* and *The Topical Times Football Annuals*. Both would be packed with black and white photographs of players, airbrushed to make them look as though they were in colour. The airbrushing technique had its most marked effect on the players' faces, making them all look like inscrutable North Koreans. It also made the detail of the spectators in the crowds disappear entirely, leaving the impression that the likes of Danny Blanchflower or Tom Finney were demonstrating their skills before an orange blur.

In amongst the socks, liquorice smokers' sets and chocolate joiners' outfits, whose chocolate was always inferior to Cadbury's and would congeal and stick to the roof of your mouth, would be a diary.

For me, it was always *Lett's Legible Football Diary for Boys*, with its pale blue pages and blue rinse photographs of the previous year's internationals and Cup final. The title of the diary was always a source of wonder to me. Did they really produce an illegible version? I'd pore over such books for hours on end, every player a hero to me. Little did I think that in the space of a few years, it would be me who would be featuring so frequently within the pages.

When I became a player, Christmas games had a magic all of their own. The crowd rustled in their new clothes and the usual match aroma of Park Drives, Bovril and pies that wafted down from the stands and terraces carried more than a hint of cigar.

The football fixtures were arranged so that clubs would not be engaged in local derbies as such, but would at least play a team within easy travelling distance. Boxing Day attendances were always amongst the largest of the season. The powers that be worked on the assumption that by the time Boxing Day afternoon had come around, most people had had enough of family life indoors and would give their eye teeth to get out of the house, irrespective of the weather.

The options were the pantomime or the match. For most, it was the match, and if your team was playing away, then there was always the consolation that it was not too far away. If all went well, you would be sitting down to the remains of the turkey by 6.30 in the evening, whilst the kids watched the black and white telly through a transparent Quality Street wrapper, wondering if this was what colour TV would be like.

United made a short trip north to Blackburn Rovers during the festive period in 1965. It was a bitterly cold day and the Ewood Park pitch was so icy that Matt Busby joked we'd have trouble turning around at half-time without landing on our arses. The huge crowd had little to cheer and warm them as the two teams struggled to come to terms with both the frozen pitch and a bitterly cold wind which came in from the Irish Sea. At half-time, both sets of players gingerly tottered off the field with hardly a shot having been fired in anger.

In the warmth of the changing room, Matt Busby offered words of advice to Nobby about the Blackburn inside forward Andy MacEvoy. 'He puts himself about where the boots are flying, Nobby. He bends and gets his head to the ball, expecting his head to be kicked off. Don't disappoint him!'

Matt turned to me. 'George, with all your pace, you should be murdering their defence.'

'It's hard to stay upright, boss,' I replied. 'The pitch is like ice.'

'He's right, boss,' Nobby said. 'Moses couldn't part that defence.'

The buzzer sounded for us to retake the pitch. 'All you have to do is get the ball, George,' Matt said, an arm around my shoulder. 'Then run at that defence. Take them all on! Beat them and stick the bloody ball in the net. Then we can all go home and enjoy what's left of Christmas.'

When I ran back out on to the pitch for the second half, the weather seemed to be even colder. I literally skated past centre forward David Herd. 'Get the ball out wide to me straight from the kick-off, will you?' I told him. As David and Denis Law stood over the ball I could see from my position wide on the right-hand touchline that they were in conversation. The referee blew his whistle and David flicked the ball to Denis, who then hammered it hard and low out to me on the right wing.

I took off like I was running from a bush fire, on my toes all the time to get maximum speed. Fred Pickering, the Rovers centre forward, came across to cover but my pace took me past him.

Rovers' left half, Mick McGrath, was next to show. I flicked the ball to his right as he approached, veered around the other side to his left, collected the ball again and he was gone. Big Matt

Woods came across and I dropped my left shoulder as I swerved inside. Glancing up, I could see I was still some twenty-five yards from the Rovers goal but I decided to go it alone and take my chances. A blue and white shirt appeared to my right but I accelerated and left it in my wake. I knew the Rovers defence were happy to let me run to the edge of the penalty area before starting the serious stuff. A few yards from the edge of the box they held their line, so I thought my only option was to flick the ball over the top of them and carry on running.

I burst through the line, their captain, Ronnie Clayton, breathing down my neck and goalkeeper, Harry Leyland, advancing quickly. Aware that Leyland would be looking for the first indication that I was about to shoot, I made a jerking movement with my left shoulder. In such situations, goalkeepers have only a split second to make up their minds what they are going to do.

Leyland spread himself across the ground to restrict my view of the goal. I swerved to my right and a split second before Clayton's tackle came in, I hit the ball from an acute angle into the far corner of the net.

I turned, arm held aloft, and saw the United fans massed at the far end of the ground, bobbing up and down as they celebrated with me. Behind me, there was silence. Suddenly, a lone voice rose from the Blackburn fans jam-packed behind the goal. 'Thous't can come and play for't Rovers any time, Bestie, lad!' the voice hollered.

I turned to where I thought the voice had come from in the crowd and mouthed the words 'thank you', then took a little bow. The terraces behind the goal broke into spontaneous applause.

Of all the wonderful things people have written and said about me, I'll never forget the words of that Rovers supporter. Today, when a player from a visiting team scores, he is usually greeted with a sea of two-fingered gestures if he is near the home terraces. In the sixties, they appreciated good football, irrespective of which side it came from. As far as I was concerned, for that

101

Rovers supporter to shout those words after I had danced my way through his team was praise indeed. Back in the dressing room at the end of the game, Matt Busby and his assistant were cock-a-hoop with the 1–0 win.

'Well done, George,' Matt said. 'You got the ball, took them all on and beat them. Then crowned it by sticking it in the onion bag. Wonderful!'

'All thanks to you, boss,' I told him.

'Thanks to me? What do you mean?' Matt asked, puzzled.

'Well, it was you who told me what to do,' I replied in all truthfulness.

Matt smiled and shook his head slowly from side to side as he turned away.

Jimmy Murphy came up as I sat sipping my tea. 'When they had us under all that pressure in the last five minutes, it was very sporting of you to go and fetch the ball for them for that free kick, seeing as Nobby had just kicked it away to try to waste some time,' he said.

'The Rovers supporters thought so too,' I said. 'They gave me a round of applause.'

'Your sportsmanship brought us a bit of luck, George,' Murphy went on. 'The ball deflating like that just after the free kick was taken and the game having to be stopped. It knocked them out of their rhythm and took the pressure off us.'

I nodded in agreement.

'Where is it?' Jimmy asked after a few moments, extending a plump hand towards me. I handed Jimmy the valve I had taken out of the original match ball when I went to retrieve Nobby's kick.

'Thanks. I always like to have a few spare,' said Jimmy stuffing it into his tracksuit pocket. 'Merry Christmas, George.'

Fans

'A fan is a person who, when you have made
an idiot of yourself on the pitch, doesn't think
you've done a permanent job.'

Francis Lee, former Manchester City player.

'A real football fan is one who knows the
nationality of every player in Jack Charlton's
Irish team.'

Les Scott

21

Fans and Adulation

I N 1969, everything was going my way. The previous year I had helped United lift the European Cup. We were in Europe again to defend it, handily placed in the League for another tilt at the Championship and competing in the World Club Championship against Estudiantes from Argentina.

I was earning something in the region of £1,000 to £1,500 a week, which in those days was a fortune. This income was made up of my wages at United, revenue from my boutiques, a three-year modelling contract with Great Universal Stores and numerous advertising and product-endorsement contracts. Remember the slogan, 'E for B and be your Best' from the TV commercial for the Egg Marketing Board?

I had been voted the European Footballer of the Year and English Footballer of the Year. My face appeared on the covers of magazines as diverse as *Football Monthly*, *Life*, *Woman*, *Paris Match*, *New Society* and the *Tiger* comic. It seemed everyone was interested in me.

It was all too much for a twenty-three-year-old to cope with, especially as I had to handle nearly all the business side myself. In those days, the only agents belonged to Littlewoods. I couldn't walk down a street without being mobbed and the adulation became ridiculous. When I went to a private clinic for some tests on my right knee and hip, I was told to go into a room and get undressed so that a nurse could examine me. When I found the room, the nurse was behind a screen. Looking around, I couldn't see a chair or hanger for my clothes. 'Where shall I put my clothes?' I asked.

'On top of mine,' the nurse replied as she came from behind the screen, totally naked!

The first time I felt the enthusiasm of the fans was becoming absurd was in 1966 in the quarter-final of the European Cup against Benfica. Benfica's home is called the Stadium of Light and is a wonderful place to play. The atmosphere is electric and the multi-tiered stands that wrap themselves around the ground seem to reach up into the heavens.

We had won the first leg at Old Trafford 3–2 and press pundits wondered if we had done enough at home to survive the away leg. On the night we produced what many believe to be one of the greatest performances by a British side in Europe. Benfica had not been beaten at home for six years and we swept them aside, winning 5–1. I scored two, with Bobby Charlton, John Connelly and Pat Crerand netting one each.

I had started the game feeling very confident and set about taking the Benfica defence apart. The rest of the team caught the mood and when half-time came we were 3–0 up and Benfica had lost their heart.

At the end of the game, the Portuguese fans were chanting, 'El Beatle', likening me to the Fab Four because of the way I wore my hair. As I walked off the pitch, one of the Benfica fans climbed over the fencing and ran across the pitch towards me. At first I thought he was coming across to pat me on the back and it was only when he was a couple of yards away that I realised he was brandishing a butcher's knife in his hand!

I shouted out to Denis Law and goalkeeper Harry Gregg, who were nearest to me, and they rushed to my aid as I started to grapple with the fan. Quite a struggle ensued before Harry managed to wrestle the knife from the fan's hand just as the police intervened. I was terrified, the fan was screaming at me in Portuguese and Harry and Denis looked on in bewilderment as the police started to laugh.

'No need for concern,' one of the policemen said as his colleagues frogmarched the screaming fan away. 'He only wanted to cut a piece of your hair as a souvenir. He likes you, really he does.'

'He wanted a lock of your hair?' said Harry jokingly. 'If I were you I'd have given him the whole wig!'

The groundsman at Old Trafford was a wonderful, warm man called Joe Royle. Joe was head groundsman at United for over fifty years and in that time had numerous assistants and helpers. I always stopped and passed the time of day with Joe and one day, in 1969, he told Denis Law and me about an incident which had happened the year before concerning one of his assistants, Jimmy Taylor.

Jimmy was in his mid-twenties and a United fanatic who would not only watch first team games, but reserve and youth team matches as well. If a United team of any status was playing, Jimmy was there. Joe used to joke that when the laundry ladies hung the United shirts out on the line, Jimmy would have paid two bob just to watch them dry.

Jimmy loved United and, according to Joe, was my biggest fan. He had pasted photographs of me all over the walls of the shed that housed the mowers and groundsman's equipment. Joe said Jimmy's house was just the same: photographs of me adorned the walls of nearly every room.

Jimmy lived in a terraced house not far fom Old Trafford and one Friday evening, Joe called to ask him if he would come in a little earlier the next morning to work on the pitch, which had been subjected to a lot of rain. When there was no answer at the front door, Joe decided to walk round to the rear of the house via the back lane. The houses were

divided at the back by low walls and as Joe approached the back gate, he had a clear view into the lounge at the rear of the house.

What he saw took him aback. Jimmy's wife was kissing and cuddling another man on the settee and passions were running high. Joe, forever the gentleman, made a discreet retreat and headed back to his own home. He told Denis and I that all that night he turned the incident over and over in his mind, wondering whether or not to tell Jimmy about his wife's infidelity.

The next morning when Jimmy turned up for work, Joe was in a dilemma. Should he tell or not? Joe didn't want to see Jimmy hurt or made a fool of; then again, he felt it was not up to him to get involved in a domestic dispute.

As the morning wore on Joe toyed with his plight. As the two sat down to eat their sandwiches in their hut at lunchtime, Joe felt he had to try to make Jimmy aware that something was going on behind his back, and in his own home, at that. After skirting the issue for ten minutes or so, Jimmy took the bull by the horns, so to speak.

'Jimmy,' he said very seriously. 'I know something that I think you should know.'

'Like what?' Jimmy asked, munching on his sandwiches, unconcerned.

'You may well feel that I have no business telling you this and you're probably right,' Joe said. 'But I have some very bad news for you, Jimmy. The thing is, you'd find out about it sooner or later, so as your boss and your friend, I think you'd rather hear it from me.'

'Hear what?' Jimmy said, now anxious and fretting.

His voice grave and serious, Joe told Jimmy how he had called at his home the previous night and seen his wife in a passionate embrace with another man.

For a few seconds, there was silence in the groundsman's hut.

'Is that all?' Jimmy said eventually, his voice buoyant with relief. 'I thought you were going to tell me George Best wasn't playing today 'cos he were injured.'

22

A Fervent Fan

Not long after our European Cup success at United in 1968, Denis Law and I went for a night out in Manchester city centre. We didn't want to be out too late, so we followed a few drinks with a visit to an Italian restaurant.

We had left our cars at home with the intention of catching a taxi back because we knew we'd be drinking. We left the restaurant at around 11.10 but had little success in finding a cab. Walking down Portland Street, we noticed a number of buses stationed by the depot in Sackville Street ready for use first thing in the morning.

'What time is it?' Denis asked.

I told him it was now going on for 11.30.

'The Bramall bus runs from here,' Denis said. 'Come on, we might catch the last one.'

'We ran over to another line of buses parked at the depot entrance and were frantically looking for one that had Bramall on the front when we spotted a driver knocking off for the night. 'What time does the last bus to Bramall go?' I asked him.

'Oh, you two lads are too late for that,' the driver said. 'Last bus t'Bramall left five minutes ago.'

We thanked him and were turning away to search the empty streets for a taxi when the driver suddenly called out. 'Hey, wait a minute! You're George Best and Denis Law, aren't you?'

We agreed that we were.

'Bloody 'ell, I watch thee both every 'ome game!' the driver said. 'Think you're both fantastic.'

It transpired that this driver had been an ardent United fan since he was a small boy, so we chatted for a couple of minutes about the recent European Cup victory. 'Are you both really headed for Bramall?' the driver asked.

'Yes,' I said.

'Bramall?' he repeated. 'I've just finished my shift and parked my bus for the night. Come on, I'll start it up again and run you both home.'

'No, no,' said Denis. 'It's very kind of you, but we wouldn't want to put you to so much trouble.'

'It's no trouble at all,' the driver insisted. 'In fact, it would be an honour. It would be really something to tell my kids when they grow up – that their dad gave George Best and Denis Law a lift home in his bus.'

Denis and I attempted to dissuade the driver from his kind offer, but to no avail. The more we tried to decline, the more insistent he became about running us home. 'What the hell,' I said to Denis eventually. 'Let's take the bus home.'

We followed the driver over to a single-decker bus and he opened the doors and invited us to step aboard. Denis and I sat together near the front as the driver brought the engine to life. It was the strangest feeling to be the only passengers, especially as we were sitting in the dark – the driver didn't want to risk detection by putting on the interior lights.

The bus started to pull out into Sackville Street, when suddenly we were waved to a halt by an irate bus inspector. He walked around to the cab side and our driver pulled down his window.

'Where the hell do you think you're going?'

'Bramall,' the driver told him.

'Bramall? That's an unscheduled run!' the inspector said, checking the papers on his clipboard.

'I know,' our driver said. 'I've got George Best and Denis Law on board. They've missed their last bus home and as I've just finished a shift, I thought I'd take them.'

The inspector stared in disbelief. 'Just hold this bus here,' he ordered and then walked around the cab front and climbed on board.

Standing at the top of the steps he shone a torch on Denis and me. We sat there very sheepishly, not knowing what we could do to help our Good Samaritan.

'Take this bus back into the depot immediately,' the inspector ordered, staring at Denis and me.' And take out a double-decker. They might want to smoke.'

23

Wally Stoddart

WALLY Stoddart had supported Manchester United since before the First World War. When I was playing for the club, Wally would always hang around in the car park, collecting autographs. Rain, wind or shine, he was there with a red Silvine exercise book and a large sugar-paper scrapbook containing photographs of United players and games, cut from football magazines and newspapers. Every season, a new scrapbook would appear. He must have been in his seventies when I came across him, but he still had a boyish enthusiasm for Manchester United and thought every player was a god.

At the start of the 1968–69 season United had been involved in a disappointing 2–2 home draw with West Bromich Albion and goalkeeper Alex Stepney, normally a wonderful, warm and thoughtful player who always had time for the supporters, was feeling down because he believed he was at fault for one of the Albion goals.

Wally thought the sun shone out of Alex's backside, especially after Alex's tremendous performance in goal during our 1968 European Cup victory over Benfica when, with the score at 1–1 and extra time looming, Alex made a brave point-blank save at the feet of Eusebio to keep us in the game.

On the day of the Albion game, Wally had his grandson with him and had been delighting the small boy with tales of Alex's heroics. As Alex left the players' entrance and made his way to his car, he was still seething about Albion's second goal. Wally, seeing his hero emerge, pushed his grandson towards him. The small boy, who was probably six or seven years of age, tottered towards Alex holding an autograph book and pen above his head.

'Go on,' said Walter encouragingly, 'Say what I told you to say.'

''Scuse me, can I have your autograph, please?' the small boy said in a croaky voice.

'Piss off!' Alex said uncharacteristically, his mind still on the Albion goal.

The boy turned and tottered back towards old Wally, bewildered.

'Did you hear what he said to you?' Wally said, smiling and laughing. 'Didn't your grandad tell you Stepney was a great character?'

The tales about old Wally's passion for Manchester United are legendary. The story goes that one day Wally was walking to Old Trafford for a home game when a funeral cortege passed by. Wally stopped, took off his cap and bowed his head. Once the procession of funeral cars had passed, a fellow United fan who had witnessed Wally's actions complimented him.

That was a very respectful thing you did back there, the other fan said to Wally as they continued their walk towards Old Trafford.

The very least I could do,' said Wally. 'I was married to her for forty years.'

The Managers

'At twenty enthusiasm reigns, at thirty the wit and at forty the judgement.'

Sir Matt Busby, Manchester United.

'Very few players have the courage of my convictions.'

Brian Clough, former manager of Nottingham Forest.

24

The Boss

MATT BUSBY was class. Not part of a certain class, you understand – Matt was in a class of his own. He was a player of considerable note with Manchester City and Liverpool between 1929 and 1945, but it is with Manchester United that his name will be forever synonymous. He first took over the reigns at Old Trafford in 1945, and from then until his retirement in 1969, he elevated his position as football manager to one of statesman. He was a father figure to me and I loved him dearly. In his time, he created three really great United teams: the side that won the FA Cup in 1948, the Busby Babes of the fifties, and the European Cup-winning side of the sixties, of which I was privileged to be a member.

He was an innovator in that he pioneered European football, pressing the Football League to allow English teams to participate in the European competitions that were being formed in the mid 1950s. This coincided with the creation of the team that bore the legendary name 'Busby Babes', a team that was to experience tragedy when twenty-three people, including eight United players, lost their lives in the Munich air disaster of 1958. Matt himself was fortunate to survive that tragedy, but survive he did, and along with his assistant, Jimmy Murphy, he created another great side, the United team I played in, and we went on to bring him the League Championship and his Holy Grail, the European Cup.

Some say that Matt had no stomach for confrontation; that certain players, myself included, got away with too much. The fact of the matter is that Matt didn't bawl you out because he didn't have to. He'd prepare the ground so cleverly that players often talked themselves out of the side to make way for a replacement Matt wanted to bring in. Shouting and bawling was beneath the man's dignity.

In February 1968, United visited White Hart Lane and came off second-best to a typically strong Spurs side, losing 3–0. We sat in silence in the dressing room after the game. No one attempted to get stripped and into the bath. To a man, we sat sipping our tea, still showing the dirt and sweat of battle.

Suddenly, the dressing-room door opened and in walked Matt, resplendent in a navy blue suit, white shirt and club tie. I expected him to examine our performance and berate certain individuals for giving Spurs players like Jimmy Greaves and Jimmy Robertson too much room and freedom. To this day I remember that it was so quiet, I could hear his black shoes creaking as he circled the room, eyeing each of us whilst fingering his chin with the thumb and forefinger of his right hand.

He paused in front of goalkeeper Alex Stepney. 'How do you think you played today, Alex?' Matt asked, calm and collected.

'I've conceded three goals, but I thought I played OK, boss,' Alex told him throatily.

Matt said nothing. He just murmured to himself and moved on to right back Shay Brennan. 'And you, Shay? How do you think you've performed today?'

'To be honest boss, I don't think I played that badly at all,' Shay informed the boss and the rest of the room.

More silence. Matt circled the room again and stopped in front of big Bill Foulkes, our centre half. 'Bill?'

'I did all right. 'Fact I reckon if I hadn't been on my mettle, we might have lost by more than three,' Bill said confidently. The boss stood for a moment or two and said nothing, before moving on again. 'And you Denis?'

'I thought I played OK, boss,' Denis Law said matter-of-factly.

'And what sort of game do you reckon you had, Bobby?'

Bobby Charlton said he thought he'd played all right in the middle of the park and that none of Spurs' three goals could be put down to him.

The boss then turned and asked me the same question.

'I created plenty and with a bit more luck I think we could have had a couple of goals,' I replied, feeling a little intimidated but wanting to express my opinion.

The boss continued to walk slowly around the room until he had put his question to every player. Each thought he had played well.

Matt stood in the middle of the room and placed his hands behind his back. He was facing Nobby Stiles, and it was then that I realised Nobby was the only player he had not spoken to.

Eventually, after about thirty seconds elapsed in total silence, the boss spoke again, slowly and deliberately. 'And what of you Nobby? How have you played today?'

No sooner had he asked the question than Nobby jumped to his feet. 'Well I must have been shit, mustn't I?' he squawked. 'Everyone else has had a good game, yet we lost three-nil. So I must have been bloody hopeless!'

The boss never said a word. He turned on his heels and walked slowly out of the room.

For our next game against West Ham at Old Trafford, Nobby was dropped.

25

Danny Boy

SIR MATT didn't spend much time giving team talks. More often than not I didn't bother going into the dressing room when it was time for his talk. I'd be off down the corridor making myself a cup of tea, or chatting to friends in the foyer entrance. A reporter from the *Daily Mail* once asked Matt why he didn't insist on me being present at his team talks. 'Because my team talk is always the same,' he informed the scribe. 'I just say, give the ball to George.'

Matt's approach was in sharp contrast to the style of the other two managers I had particular experience of, Danny Blanchflower and Billy Bingham, who managed the Northern Ireland teams I played for. Matt would get his points across quickly and succinctly. Billy Bingham was knowledgeable, but somewhat long-winded when it came to telling a team what he wanted them to do. But even Billy was the prince of précis compared to the dear, departed Danny Blanchflower.

Danny was a lovely man, but his team talks couldn't have lasted longer if he had been reading us *Gone With the Wind*. I just wanted to get out on to the pitch and get on with it. Danny felt every player had to be given a sermon in order to do that.

Danny is no longer with us and football is all the poorer for it, but he left me many fond memories. He would wax lyrical about football and its relation to life. Football and its relation to endeavour. Football and its relation to a canteen cup. To ask him anything about football was to invite a reply as epic as one of Milton's poems. No matter what sort of question reporters fired at Danny during the post-match press conferences, he'd field them with the ease and certitude of Nasser Hussain in the covers.

Much is written about the wit and wisdom of Shankly, Clough and Atkinson, but little about Danny's. It's a pity, for in amongst the seemingly endless discourse, you would be treated to some sparkling gems (if your attention span had the stamina). Danny was easy-going, always philosophising, always articulate and witty. A reporter once asked him about me. Most managers would have replied with a list of insipid superlatives, not so Danny.

'George makes a greater appeal to the senses than Finney or Matthews did,' Danny said. 'His movements are quicker, lighter, more balletic. He offers grander surprises to the mind and the eye. He has ice in his veins, warmth in his heart and timing and balance in his feet.'

The reporter looked up from his notebook, somewhat agitated. 'Yes, Danny,' he said, pencil poised, 'but do you rate George as a player?'

In a world where most managers are Tabloid Tommies, Danny was Soccer's Shakespeare, an Oscar Wilde of Wembley and Windsor Park. He once asked the Northern Ireland right back John Parke how things were going back at his club, Sunderland. John told him they were worried they wouldn't escape relegation this time around.

'Worry,' said Danny, 'is the interest you pay on trouble before it comes. You have ten matches to go. That's twenty points to go for. Avoid trouble!'

Danny once asked for players' opinions about our style of play prior to a game against Russia. Dundee's Billy Campbell, whose work rate Danny always felt could be better, came up with an idea that would considerably change our pattern of play. Danny listened quietly and intently. When Billy had finished, he calmly stepped forward. 'Thank you, Billy,' he said. 'I feel you would do well to remember that ideas are very funny things. They never work unless you do.'

Danny had taken a cottage not far from the town of Newtownards, which nestles at the edge of the beautiful Strangford Loch six miles east of Belfast. I was with Manchester United on a pre-season tour in 1965 when Danny invited my fellow Northern Ireland international Jimmy Nicholson and I to visit him for tea one afternoon.

In those days you could catch a train from Belfast and Danny gave me the instructions to his cottage over the phone at United's hotel. Having been given permission by Matt Busby to go, Jimmy Nicholson and I set off, following Danny's instructions. Once we got into Newtownards, we were to take a branch line train to the village. Danny's rented cottage was right in the centre, opposite the village's only pub-come-hotel. It was, he informed me, simply a matter of turning left when we came out of the station and walking down the road to the house.

On arriving at the branch line station Jimmy and I immediately turned left and walked down a lane flanked by high hedges. After about ten minutes, Jimmy expressed his concern that I had misheard Danny's instructions about turning left out of the station. I was adamant I had heard correctly. We carried on walking, and every time we came to a bend, we thought the village must be just around the corner. Eventually it was – some three miles from the station.

In the one-street village we found Danny's cottage with no problem. He opened the door and welcomed Jimmy and I like long-lost sons. As we sat down to tea, Danny asked if we had had a pleasant journey from Belfast.

I told him we had, but the walk from the station to the village was a bit longer than we had expected.

'It's a fair walk, true enough.' Danny said. 'I've done it

myself many times. It's just over three miles.' He poured out more tea.

'Danny,' I asked, somewhat puzzled, 'why on earth, when they were building the station, did they not put it *in* the village?'

Danny thought for a moment. 'A good point, George,' he said. 'As a matter of fact, when they decided to build the station they did talk about putting it in the centre of the village. But then it was decided it would be better if it were next to the railway line.'

26

Taking Stock

HE spanned the two eras of football since the war: from when all teams played to a 'W' formation and the period from the early sixties onwards when teams lined up in 4–4–2 or 4–4–3 formation, depending on what system a manager preferred. He was a manager prior to England's rude awakening in the fifties at the hands of Continental opposition and he continued to manage up to and far beyond the winning of the World Cup in 1966.

Alec Stock never looked like a manager who belonged to either era. During the forties and fifties football managers looked much the same as they did pre-war. Dressed in sombre suits, watch and chain hanging from waistcoat pocket, and sporting a trilby, they appeared cheerless and funereal, like a local magistrate or school inspector. Such managers were always referred to as 'Mr' and the club programme took great delight in listing all the initials of their Christian names, giving them the dusty formality of Victorian cricketers.

When managers as prim as quakers gave way in the late fifties to the then England manager Walter Winterbottom's tracksuit manager we know today, Alec Stock remained untouched. Beneath tweed jacket or light sports coat he'd wear a crisp white shirt, the collar open, his cravat billowing out like a June rose in full bloom. In light cavalry twill trousers and brown brogues, polished so well they looked as if they were made of glass, Alec looked more like the director of the local amateur dramatic society or a poet than a worldly-wise football man. It was fitting, because in many ways, the words he spoke, the ideas he nurtured were indeed sheer poetry.

At the onset of his managerial career, Alec broke the mould. In the days when the only fast food was stewed prunes and 2.30 was the time the match kicked off and not how much it cost to watch the reserves, Alec amazed everyone when he joined Yeovil Town in 1949 and announced he was to be a 'player-manager'. It was as if a lathe-turner from the factory floor had suddenly announced he was the company's new MD and would combine both roles.

Yeovil were a non-league outfit, but not without substance, and under the young Alec's guiding hand they produced probably the most famous win in their history. In 1949, they knocked a star-studded Division One Sunderland side out of the FA Cup – Len Shackleton, Johnny Mapson and all. The directors of Yeovil Town, who had the courage to agree to Alec's demand for the previously unheard-of position of player-manager, sat back and puffed on cigars the size of chair legs in the smug satisfaction that they had appointed someone whose talent equated with their considerable ambition.

It was Alec's first taste of success as a manager and thrust him immediately into the limelight. Outside the ground, hundreds of Town fans unable to get into the match had listened to Raymond Glendenning's BBC Radio commentary on police car radios, doors open and volume turned up full. With a minute remaining and Yeovil leading 2–1, Sunderland won a free kick just outside Town's penalty area. As the Sunderland left back prepared to have a go in a last-ditch effort to save face, Alec lined up his defensive wall. 'Right,' he said through gritted teeth, 'if anyone ducks out of the way of this, you're sacked!'

Jackie Stelling, Sunderland's number 3, drilled the ball into the defensive wall and immediately the line-up disintegrated as all five members descended upon the loose ball. No one knows for sure who made contact with the ball and who didn't – perhaps it was all five simultaneously because the ball took off like a comet over the roof of the main stand and was never seen again. For all I know it may still be going.

From those formative days, Alec was to carve out a career in which he won the admiration and respect of every player he handled. Talk to those who played under him at Fulham, QPR, Luton or Bournemouth, and the consensus of opinion is that Alec was one of the best. He may have had the admiration of the players and, for that matter, the fans, but for some reason, Alec never managed one of the really big clubs.

There are some who say he was never offered one of the top jobs; others hold that he was, but politely declined, content to wheel and deal, sign and sell, create and cultivate teams made up of the eccentrics, ne'er-do-wells and honest journeymen.

With the odd exception, Alec's teams did not carry big-name players, yet he always created teams which played flowing, attractive football. It was his ability to mould and shape a bunch of players who were not individually outstanding into an attractive, capable team that made Alec what he was. A team is a reflection of its manager and Alec's were honest, endeavouring, stylish, entertaining and cosmopolitan.

Alec travelled far and wide in search of players for his teams. It is doubtful whether there was another manager at the time who possessed Alec's knowledge of players from lower divisions and the reserve sides of the top-name clubs.

A reporter once happened across the dapper Alec sitting alone in the stand watching a reserve match at Fulham one January afternoon. 'Who have you come to watch?' the reporter asked.

'No one,' replied Alec with a sigh.

'Well, you must have made the journey to see a player from one of the sides,' the reporter insisted.

Alec, sitting cross-legged with one arm lazily draped across the back of the empty seat next to him, shook his head slowly.

The reporter, sensing he might be on to a story, pressed on. 'Managers don't come and watch Fulham reserves for no reason at all,' he said.

'I do,' Alec said. 'If you can spend a perfectly useless afternoon in a perfectly useless manner, you have learned how to live.' He gave the newsman a lazy, dismissive wave of his right hand.

The reporter, for his part unable to penetrate Alec's defensive wall or think of a follow-up line, beat a retreat, leaving Alec the sole person in Fulham's main stand.

A week later one of the Fulham reserves signed for Alec at QPR. His name was Rodney Marsh.

27

Man Management and
Transfer Talk

MATT BUSBY was not only one of the greatest football
managers of all time, he was a leader of vision and
distinction. Above all, Matt knew that leadership was action
and not just position. He led from the front and did so with
verve, confidence, dignity and grace.

Under Matt's guidance, Manchester United won the European
Cup in 1968, the League Championship five times, in 1952, 1956,
1957, 1965 and 1967, and two FA Cups, in 1948 and 1963.
They might well have made it four but for the tragic Munich
air disaster. They lost out in the finals in 1957 and 1958 against
Aston Villa and Bolton Wanderers respectively.

Matt wanted us, as players, to have a complete understanding
with one another on the pitch. That achieved, he created a
pattern of play based upon our individual talents. 'When we
have the ball,' he used to tell us, 'we are all attackers. When
we lose the ball, we are all defenders. Now what's complicated
about that?'

We played it simple and we played to our strengths. I was
good at dribbling and taking players on, so that's what I was
encouraged to do. Matt ensured that the players behind me fed
me the sort of ball I needed to do just that.

There was a hard side to Matt, as the board found out when

they appointed him manager in 1945. He was a thirty-five-year-old who had just been demobbed from the Army, where he had been a company sergeant-major. Matt demanded he be free from boardroom interference and allowed to make all his own decisions. Such implicit belief in his own ability in many ways advanced the emancipation of the football manager from the almost feudal way directors treated them in those days.

As far as I know, Matt only had one bitterness where Manchester United was concerned. It is alleged that, for years, Louis Edwards, the chairman and a long-time friend of Matt's, intimated that, in time, both their sons would be 'looked after' by being made directors at Old Trafford.

Louis Edwards' son, Martin, did become a director and not only succeeded his father as chairman but today sits on top of the United empire as the club's highly salaried chief executive. However, Matt's son, Sandy, never got to be a director.

It could be this disappointment that prompted Matt to oppose the share issue that made Martin Edwards the figurehead at Old Trafford. That said, what supporters don't know is that Martin Edwards arranged for Matt to be the beneficiary of the former Red Devils' souvenir shop at Old Trafford as a reward for what he had achieved for the club. The revenue from this would have more than 'looked after' Sandy, albeit indirectly.

There are some who say that Matt could have dealt with me better when I went astray and that if he had, my career would have continued. Hindsight is a wonderful thing, but the fact of the matter is that Matt's man-management was very good. It worked with just about every other player, so why not me? Looking back, I think it was all down to the fact that I was the first of what might be called the 'superstar players'. I was a child of the time: the swinging sixties of pop music, sexual liberation and fashion. No player in the history of the game had ever previously experienced such exposure to the media.

I owned boutiques; top fashion designers wanted me to model

their clothes; the press called me the 'fifth Beatle'. Matt didn't relate to it at all, and consequently, when I had problems handling the fame and adulation, he could not come up with the right advice. This is not meant as a criticism of Matt, it is just the way it was.

Matt's man-management of other players, however, was excellent and sometimes, a treat to behold. When I first joined United they had a wing half called Mark 'Pancho' Pearson, so called because of his Zapata-style moustache. Mark was a colourful character to say the least, and one who felt he should be in the first team more often than he was. Matt, however, felt Mark's passing was not what it should be and often preferred to play someone like Nobby Lawton, whom he believed was a better distributor of the ball.

Not to be outdone, Mark practised and practised his passing. When training was over for the day, he would persuade a junior like myself to stay behind with him for the afternoon and help him work on his game. After a few weeks, Mark played for the reserves in a Central League game at Old Trafford against Everton which was watched by Matt. Following the game, Mark approached Matt in the players' lounge. 'Notice any difference, boss?' he asked optimistically.

Matt turned to Mark and gave him one of his long, thoughtful looks. 'You've trimmed that stupid moustache!' he said, as Mark paled.

In 1966, I spent a large part of the season out of the game following a cartilage operation on my right knee. Matt went out and bought John Connelly from Burnley to replace me. John was a very talented winger who was to play in the early matches of England's World Cup triumph of 1966 before losing out to Alan Ball. A true sportsman, John probably never committed a foul in his entire playing career.

Matt liked that in a player, but he also looked for the other qualities that made a winner. Following John's signing, Matt took him to one side prior to a game against Liverpool at Old Trafford. 'Happy to be here?' he enquired.

'Oh yes, Mr Busby,' John replied. 'Very happy, and what a thrill to be playing for United against Liverpool. Two great teams who play great football.'

Matt nodded in agreement.

'I was brought up at Burnley to believe that winning isn't the be all and end all,' John continued. 'It's how the game is played that matters.'

Matt nodded again. 'Aye, that's true, son,' he said. 'Providing, of course, we beat these Scouse bastards today.'

Albert Quixall was an inside forward who had joined United from Sheffield Wednesday in 1958 and played in the side that won the FA Cup by beating Leicester City 3-1 in 1963. In his time he was a very good player, but he tried to con Matt and the crowd in the latter stages of his time at United. He had lost his pace and was unable to work as hard in matches as he once had. He tried to cover it up and would attempt to reach a ball or pass, but in so doing, would seem to slip. Eventually, after some poor performances, Matt left him out of the side and Oldham Athletic bought him. Matt was a little disappointed that a man who had been such a very good player in his time should try to con him into thinking he still had the skills to perform at the highest level. When Oldham came in for Albert, Matt let him know there'd be no one standing in his way.

'How did the talks with Oldham go?' Matt asked Albert.

'They want me to play for them very badly,' Albert said.

'Then you're just the man,' Matt told him.

One day, Matt received a call from the manager of Bristol Rovers, Bert Tann, who had heard that he was looking for an understudy centre half to Bill Foulkes, who was coming towards the end of his career. Tann had a young centre half at Rovers called David Stone whom he rated very highly. At the time Rovers were strapped for cash and Tann, seemingly under pressure from his directors to raise money from what assets he had, was trying to persuade Matt that Stone was a player for United's future. Matt wasn't convinced.

'I'll tell you this, Matt,' Tann said, his sales pitch in full flow. 'Fifty thousand wouldn't buy this lad.'

'I know,' said Matt. 'And I'm one of the fifty thousand.'

In 1962, Matt was keen to bring Denis Law back from Italy. Matt felt Denis was ideal for the system he was playing and a great player into the bargain. He had heard that although Torino were one of the biggest clubs in Europe and enjoying considerable success in Italy, Denis was unhappy with life over there. Matt had arranged via the United secretary, Les Olive, to talk on the telephone to one of the English-speaking Torino directors about the possibility of Denis moving to Old Trafford.

'If he is to return to England,' the Torino director told Matt, 'it is going to take a lot of money.'

'How much?' Matt asked.

'Two hundred thousand pounds.'

Matt was flabbergasted. Up to that point, United's record transfer was the £45,000 they had paid for Albert Quixall in 1958. 'That's too much,' he informed the director. 'We are a big club, but in England no club has that sort of money.'

'OK, how about if we say a hundred and eighty thousand pounds for Mr Law?'

'Still far too much,' Matt said.

'A hundred and sixty thousand?'

'How can I make you understand?' Matt said. 'No one in England has this sort of money.'

'A hundred and fifty thousand?'

'In English terms you're still talking silly money,' Matt told the official. 'Even if my directors had that sort of money, they wouldn't allow me to spend it on just one player, no matter how good he was.'

'A hundred and thirty thousand?'

'Still too high.'

Some ten minutes of haggling followed before the director dropped the asking price once more. 'How about a hundred and twenty thousand?'

'No,' said Matt emphatically. 'Too much.'

It was also getting too much for the Torino director, who began to lose patience with Matt. 'OK, Mr Busby,' he said, agitated. 'How much do you want to spend on Denis Law?'

'A hundred and ten thousand pounds.'

'OK, OK, we make a deal on a hundred and ten,' the director said, happy to be parting with a player who was not heart and soul behind his club's cause. 'But tell me one thing. Why do you come to the great Torino to buy players when our players are the most expensive in the world?'

'Because when it comes to bringing success to Manchester United,' said Matt, 'money is no object.'

28

Jimmy Bloomfield

SADLY, Jimmy Bloomfield is no longer with us. In the fifties and early sixties, Jimmy was a gifted winger who plied his trade with Brentford, Arsenal and Leicester City. He went into football management when his playing days were over and enjoyed reasonable success with some of football's less fashionable clubs – notably Leicester City, whom he managed from 1971 to 1977, and Leyton Orient. Jimmy managed Orient twice, from 1968 to 1971 and between 1977 and 1981, and it was in 1978, during his second spell of management at Brisbane Road, that he took the Os to the semi-finals of the FA Cup, where they narrowly lost to Arsenal.

Jimmy was intelligent, articulate and well read. He could quote Shakespeare or John Donne as well the FA Coaching Manual and this, together with a sense of humour as dry as a desert, made him a popular speaker at functions and presentations. He was a very good speaker, his only weakness being a blank spot when it came to remembering the names of people he did not know well.

In 1976, I accepted an invitation to present the end-of-season awards for the Leicestershire Senior League. There were to be two other people there to help me with the presentation: Jimmy Bloomfield and a man called Roy Hitchkiss, who, for reasons known only to himself, had been invited by the president of the league.

Roy Hitchkiss was due to make the first presentation and just as he was about to do so, the secretary of the Leicester Senior

League asked Jimmy Bloomfield to stand up and introduce him.

'Who is he?' Jimmy asked the secretary.

'I have no idea,' the secretary replied. 'The league president asked him to come along.'

'Well, haven't you got a biog. or a note saying who he is and what he's done?' asked Jimmy.

'Not a thing,' said the secretary.

Then the league president called upon Jimmy Bloomfield to stand and introduce Roy Hitchkiss to the massed hall. Jimmy rose and without hesitation launched himself confidently into the introduction.

'Mr President, ladies and gentlemen, it gives me great pleasure to come along this evening to the annual presentation of awards for the Leicestershire Senior League.'

'I am particularly delighted to have been asked to introduce a man who has a great surname, the last part of which is synonymous with love and pleasure the world over. George Villiers said such a thing was like grains of gold or silver found upon the ground, of no value in itself, but precious in showing that a mine is near. Gabriel Rosetti called them messengers of love. Polynesian women believe that to have one placed upon their lips is the first step towards a heavenly experience, whilst in mediaeval English tapestries, young girls are depicted longing for such a thing from knights returning from war. Indeed,' he went on, warming to his theme, and pleased with his resourceful ad-libbing, 'it is reputed that when our very own Queen had her first experience of one with Prince Philip, she knew it was he whom she wished to marry. And I am sure that many of you sitting out there tonight will have indulged yourselves with one at some time this day and that is why, without further ado, I would like to introduce to you now, Mr . . .'

Jimmy paused for a split second as he racked his brains for the name.

'. . . Mr Roy Hitchcock!'

29

The Debut Role

THE fifties was a time of thick cotton football shirts with stiff collars and buttons which, on a freezing day, your fingers were incapable of undoing; a time of billowing shorts and thick woollen socks that bulged from knee to boot under the strain of bamboo-cane shin pads that protruded from each stocking like a couple of editions of *War and Peace*.

The fans poured out from terraced streets where the 'leccy' men were converting daily, committing the man with the bicycle and the gas-lighting pole to the dole and memory. The homes were terraced red brick, solid and monotonous, line upon line of them. Streets that bore names of an imperialistic past, such as Mafeking, Tel-el-Kebir and Gordon, turned their backs on one another, knowing only too well that in such areas one kept one's business to oneself.

Inside, children played in front of tiled hearths and crackling coal fires with Hornby Doublo. Clocks ticked methodically and loudly, full of self-importance, and wives called 'Mother' wore . 'pinnies' and 'never had a moment' as they cooked puddings, plate pies, skirt and scrag end whilst the wireless babbled.

It was a time when you had no problem buying a Saturday evening paper in London which carried the 'classified football results'. No one knew what 'classified' meant nor indeed cared. Names such as Sherman's, Murphy's, Coral, Cope's and Empire competed every Friday with Littlewoods and Vernons for your treble-chance money.

On Radio Luxembourg, Coupeneer, Soccer Success and Horace Batchelor told you it was they who had the sure-fire system that would lead to your fortune, and it was yours for the taking, for a tanner.

Young boys knew you got cold sores if you wore short trousers in the winter, that there was a glass and a half of full cream milk in every bar of Cadbury's chocolate, that Sunderland were the Bank of England club and that a bottle of PLJ helped girls shed pounds – no diet required. It was a time when a young lad from Ashington in Northumberland by the name of Jack Charlton travelled south to Leeds and Elland Road. He was there only months before his country called upon him to do his duty.

Following his National Service, Jack returned to Elland Road in August 1956 along with another conscript. 'If I'm not in the reserves by the end of the season, I'm off,' said Jack's compatriot as they arrived back at the ground.

'Bugger that!' said Jack in his own inimitable way. 'I'm off if I'm not in the first team by Christmas!'

Which speaks volumes for Jack's motivation and determination – as it does for that of his Army pal, who was never heard of again.

It was a Leeds United pre-Don Revie, a Leeds whose hopes of success had seemingly vanished. It was surprising, for the manager at the time was one of the greatest footballers ever to have graced the game, Horatio 'Raich' Carter.

According to all who saw him, Carter was more than just special. If the midfield players of today are the engine room of a side, then the inside forwards of yesteryear were the intelligentsia who led and orchestrated the foot soldiers and artillery that went to make up a team at that time. They prodded and probed at defences, relying on brain rather than brawn. Carter was one of the best, and as a player with Sunderland in the 1930s and

1940s and later with Derby County in the early fifties, his name was synonymous with class.

After Derby County, Carter saw out his autumnal playing days at Hull City. The Humberside club had been drawn away to Sunderland in an FA Cup tie and the Roker fans gave their former favourite the sort of reception they reserve on Wearside for visiting politicians. Throughout the game, Carter was subjected to a tirade of heckling which in the main was good-humoured. The fact that Carter was not having the best of games had little to do with him. You can't play if your team-mates don't give you the ball and, on this particular day, Carter wasn't doing much because the Hull players were not winning any balls for him.

With five minutes remaining and Sunderland leading by the only goal, Hull won a corner in front of the Roker End. Amidst an aromatic fug combining Woodbines, Bovril and Craven Mints rising from behind the goal, Carter took up position at the far post. As the Hull winger was about to take the corner, a silence befell the ground, only to be broken by a lone voice from the hordes packed like sardines behind the goal. 'Get yourself back to Hull, Carter!' The voice boomed. 'You're washed up and finished!'

Good-humoured barracking is one thing, but this was going too far and the crowd shuffled their feet with embarrassment as the winger sent the ball across.

The ball was long and reached Carter at the far post. He took it on his chest and it fell at his feet. With a shimmy and a flick of his hips, he sent the Sunderland full back, Jackie Stelling, one way and the entire Roker End the other. As Ray Daniel, the home centre half, tried to close him down, Carter flicked the ball over the big Welshman's right shoulder before rounding him, then volleyed into the roof of the net. Roker Park was as silent as a country churchyard.

Suddenly, the very same voice that had just a moment before poured scorn on the great man once again broke the eerie silence.

'Well, you're not as good as you used to be!' it hollered in grudging admiration.

At Leeds it was Raich Carter who saw the promise in Jack the Lad, gave him his debut that Christmas of 1956 and in so doing offered the young Charlton some telling advice. Jack had been picked to make his debut against Doncaster Rovers and, being a raw recruit, expected Carter to be thorough in explaining the role he would have to play in the game.

For an hour leading up to the kick-off, Carter busied himself with his seasoned players and never once turned to young Jack. As the teams were about to leave the dressing room, the anxious debutant approached his manager. 'Excuse me, boss,' said Jack. 'But you haven't told me what I have to do out there.'

The great man turned slowly and placed a hand on Jack's shoulder. 'You're playing centre half, so your role is simple,' Carter informed his young charge. 'In every game you play, all you have to do is find out how quickly the opposition's centre forward can limp.'

From his very first game to his last, I reckon there are many number 9s willing to testify that Jack rarely strayed from the advice given to him by the great man.

30

Managerial Advice

I T is part of the role of a manager to offer advice, whether it be relevant to a game, an individual's play or private life. I made my debut for Manchester United in a 5–2 win over Burnley in 1963 and I can remember Matt Busby offering me a piece of advice at half-time which stayed with me for the rest of my career. I was playing on the right wing and throughout the first half had difficulty getting past the Burnley left back, Alex Elder.

'Alex, like most full backs, will match you for pace over five yards,' said Matt. 'You're running flat out as soon as you receive the ball and he's catching you over that first four or five yards. Don't try to go at breakneck speed as soon as you get the ball. Run at three-quarter speed: that way the full back adjusts his pace accordingly in order to make the tackle. Just as he commits himself, accelerate away with a burst of pace. He won't catch you then, George.'

Matt was absolutely right. In the second half I managed to beat Alex Elder more often, I scored my first League goal and helped make two more as we ran out 5–1 winners.

There are, of course, other things managers say that leave you wondering why the hell they were appointed in the first place. When Graham Taylor was manager of England, I recall him and Lawrie McMenemy saying that straight from the start of a game,

England should put the ball out for a throw-in. According to the two men best qualified to manage the English national side, England would then have an immediate advantage – when the opposition took the throw-in, they would have one player fewer than England on the field!

When Lawie McMenemy was appointed assistant England manager to Graham Taylor, a lot of eyebrows were raised. McMenemy was manager of Sunderland in 1985. In 1986, he spent most of the summer working for a television company, commentating on the World Cup in Mexico. He returned to Sunderland with only a few weeks left until the start of the 1986–87 season. Lawrie was going to have to cram in a lot of work if Sunderland were to launch a concerted challenge for promotion to Division 1, as it was then. After all, Sunderland had only just avoided relegation to Division 3 in the previous season.

Yet Lawrie seemed unconcerned. No sooner was he back on Wearside after his World Cup jaunt than he took off on a holiday to Florida. With just over a week remaining before the start of the season he got down to the job of managing Sunderland. He had no recognised goalkeeper and had to make a stop-gap on a loan signing.

The following season, Sunderland were playing in the Third Division.

As they said on Wearside at the time, McMenemy had a lot in common with the Titanic. Both were disasters, both went down and neither should have left Southampton. Lawrie left Sunderland in the middle of a very generous contract, but new chairman Bob Murray felt it was worth paying him off in favour of someone who could revive the club's fortunes. No one knows for sure how much the pay-off was, but as Tommy Docherty jokes, 'When Lawrie presented the cheque at the bank, the whole of Sunderland bounced.' Having been mainly responsible for taking a club down to the Third Division for the first time in its history, Lawrie's next job in football was assistant Manager of England!

He teamed up with Graham Taylor and the head of FA coaching, Charles Hughes, the man who, on his coaching video, begins by advising young players to ignore the way the Brazilians play football, because 'they have got it wrong'. This official FA video then goes on to expound the virtues of the long-ball game: why use eight passes to get the ball up to your forwards when you can reach them with one?

It's a far cry from the management of Matt Busby or Bill Shankly, who used to say that passing won games. More often than not, if the Manchester United team was playing well, Matt wouldn't tinker with what we had set out to do on the pitch. He'd simply pop his head around the dressing-room door at half-time and say, 'Keep playing fitba', lads.'

Neil Baker is the manager of Leek Town, and one of the best managers in the non-league game. He is surely destined to manage at League level. He is one of the new breed of managers, such as Martyn O'Neill of Wycombe Wanderers, Kenny Swain of Wigan Athletic and Chris Kinnear of Vauxhall Conference side Dover Athletic, who have fashioned sides in the lower divisions who play open and entertaining football. Neil's achievements with only a shoestring budget have been remarkable. He has lifted the club from the North-West Counties League to the brink of the Football League with a Wembley FA Trophy final appearance and FA Cup wins over Football League opposition thrown in for good measure.

Neil's knowledge of non-league footballers and eye for talent are unrivalled, and he is often asked for his opinion on semi-professional players by the scouts of Football League clubs looking to sign a possible star at a reasonable price. In 1990, Neil received a letter from Norwich City asking for his comments on a player of Italian extraction called Guido Notza, who had been scoring a few goals in non-league football with Northern Premier League club South Liverpool. Neil's reply was short but to the point: 'Guido Notza: Notza Guido!'

Matt Gillies managed Leicester City in the sixties and guided them to two FA Cup finals, in 1961 and 1963, although both were lost, to Spurs and Manchester United respectively. When any Leicester player was interviewed for TV or radio, Matt always wanted them to come across as bright and devoid of the usual insipid superlatives and footballing cliches. He felt that once a Leicester player was in front of a camera or microphone, the public would get an impression of what Leicester City was like as a club. In many respects I suppose he was right.

To create a favourable impression, Matt would take a player due to be interviewed to one side and offer advice on how to deal with the interviewer's questions. Usually this involved making some reference to a famous quote that could be applied to the type of game Leicester had been involved in that day. In 1966, Leicester City had beaten Liverpool at their home ground, Filbert Street. The BBC *Match of the Day* reporter of the time, Kenneth Wolstenholme, wanted to interview the Leicester defender John Sjoberg afterwards.

It had been a ding-dong battle of a match and as the BBC crew prepared for the interview, Matt Gillies took big John to one side. 'When Wolstenholme starts to ask you about how tough the game was, tell him that the Duke of Wellington once said that the Battle of Waterloo was won on the playing fields of Eton,' he said. 'Then tell him about how well we prepared midweek for this game against Liverpool.' John Sjoberg nodded to indicate he had understood the message.

The cameras rolled and when Wolstenholme asked John how Leicester had beaten Liverpool on the day, he tried to recall his manager's words. 'Well, you know, Duke Ellington said the Battle of Waterloo was won on the pitch at Everton,' said the burly Leicester centre half into Wolstenhome's microphone.

The interview over, Matt Gillies took big John to one side again. 'Bloody hell, John,' he said, exasperated. 'I know you're not the brightest of players, but for God's sake! Duke Ellington for the Duke of Wellington, I can understand that mistake. But how could you possibly say Everton instead of Eton?'

'I made my debut there,' said big John. 'We lost, I scored an own goal and I've hated the place ever since.'

For me, no one could equal Matt Busby when it came to gems of advice, but Matt's successor, Wilf McGuinness, would often come out with some beauties himself. In 1971, following some poor results, Wilf created quite a stir when he dropped Bobby Charlton and Denis Law from the United team for a game at Liverpool. Quizzed by the United directors about the wisdom of such a decision, Wilf had the strength of his convictions. 'I would have dropped George Best as well,' he said aggressively, 'if I could have found him.'

In 1970, I went to see Wilf McGuinness to ask his advice about a girl from a well-to-do family who lived in Wilmslow in Cheshire. I had taken the young lady in question out for a meal maybe once, certainly no more than twice, and thought nothing of it. She, however, seemed besotted with me, because she started to send expensive gifts for me to Old Trafford. I didn't want to pursue the relationship and did not return any of the many telephone calls she made to the ground. Mistakenly, I thought it would cool her advances, but the gifts continued to arrive, each one more expensive than the last as she courted my attention and approval.

People within the club started to talk and I felt I had to discuss it with Wilf otherwise I might have had a *Play Misty For Me* or *Fatal Attraction* situation on my hands. 'In the past few weeks she has sent me presents every other day or so,' I told Wilf as we sat across the desk from one another in the manager's office.

'What sort of gifts?' he asked.

I counted them on my fingers. 'A Bush record-player. Gucci shoes. An Italian suit. A gold Rolex watch. And today a car was delivered. A bloody MGB GT sports car!'

Wilf assumed an expression of concern. He put the fingertips of each hand together to form a triangle and tutted through his teeth.

'What should I do?' I asked, totally at a loss.

Wilf flopped back in his leather chair waving his right hand lazily in the air to indicate that the solution was simple. 'Send the record-player back.'

31

Shanks

A PART from the derby matches against Manchester City, the really important game of the season for me was against Liverpool. I was always one for the big occasion and they didn't come much bigger in the domestic football calendar than United against Liverpool.

For a start, you had two of the greatest post-war managers of British football pitting their wits against each other. Matt Busby and Bill Shankly both achieved a rare status reserved for the truly great by becoming legends in their own time. They were both great motivators and had that rarest of ability to spot talent. It was Shankly who spotted the potential of Ray Clemence and Kevin Keegan when they were playing Fourth Division football with Scunthorpe United. It was Matt Busby who thrust me into the United first team just after my seventeenth birthday and who signed a scrawny kid with terrible eyesight called Norbert Stiles.

It was a clash of the Titans every time the two clubs met. At United we could boast a team bristling with internationals. Likewise Liverpool. In the mid-sixties their players were household names: Ian St John, Chris Lawler, Ron Yeats, Ian Callaghan, Peter Thompson, Tony Hateley and Roger Hunt, who was a member of England's World Cup-winning team of 1966. The atmosphere when the teams met was electric. When the Liverpool Kop sang 'You'll Never Walk Alone', I'd look up from the pitch and see them swaying in time to their singing, which had the force and emotion of a massed cathedral choir.

Bill Shankly, like Matt Busby, was a canny Scot who was never lost for words. I liked him a great deal and I know he liked me. I respected his knowledge of the game and loved his keen wit, which was as sharp as legend has it. It was Shanks who, on hearing Denis Law remark that he enjoyed coming to Anfield because 'you always get a lovely cup of tea', turned to Denis and said, 'Aye, Denis son, but that's all you'll get when you come here. A cup of tea!'

After a game against Liverpool at Old Trafford in 1965, Shanks asked how I was coping with life. I was only nineteen at the time. I said things were fine with First Division football, but I was unsure about how to handle the constant media attention.

'Fame, son,' Shanks told me, 'is the price you pay for doing your job well.'

A few years later I was to understand the full implications of his words. It seemed every time I met Shanks he would come out with at least one piece of worldly wisdom or humour. When I was about to renegotiate a contract at Old Trafford and intimated that I would be looking for a considerable rise in basic pay, Shanks gave me a long, hard look. 'George, son, some advice,' he said. 'Don't be too demanding, because it's a sad fact of life that genius is born and not paid.'

He went on to tell me the story of the Liverpool full back Gerry Byrne, who, having won a place in the England team, felt he was worth considerably more than his new contract was offering. However, the way Shanks saw it, Gerry was paid for what he did for Liverpool. The fact that he had made the England team had nothing to do with what he was paid at Anfield and therefore it did not merit a rise in his wages. Gerry argued that international status was proof he had become a better player with his club.

'I may be wrong on other points, boss,' Gerry said, pressing his point. 'But I am right on this one, aren't I?'

'So what if you are?' Shanks told him. 'Even a broken clock is right twice in a day.'

Following a game against Southampton at Anfield, a young reporter from the *Southern Evening Echo* collared Shanks to ask him what he thought about a young Southampton winger called Mick Channon. Shanks was polite and told the reporter he thought the young Channon was a very good winger indeed.

'Would you say he's as good a player as Stan Matthews?' the reporter asked.

'Oh, aye,' Shankly said earnestly. 'As a player he's definitely on a par with Stan Matthews.'

The reporter thanked Shanks for his time and turned away, scribbling the quote into his notebook. Suddenly, Shanks reached out and caught the young man by the arm. 'This Channon is as good a player as Stan Matthews,' he said, 'but what you have to remember is that Stan is sixty-five now.'

In 1967, we arrived at Anfield to play Liverpool and as I glanced out of the window of the coach I saw Bill Shankly standing at the main entrance. I was the first player to alight from the coach and when I reached the entrance Bill shook my hand warmly. 'Good to see you again, George,' he said. 'You're looking well, son.'

This was unusual for him, and knowing Shanks to be a wily old fox, I decided to hang around to try to find out what he was up to. As each of the United players entered Anfield, Shanks shook his hand, welcomed him and told him how well he looked. Eventually, Bobby Charlton, a born worrier, came up to Shanks.

'Bobby, son. Good to see you,' Shanks said, shaking his hand. 'But by God, if ever there was a man who looked ill, it's you, Bobby!'

Bobby's face went as colourless as an icicle. 'Ill? I look ill?' he repeated, running the fingers of his right hand over his forehead and down his right cheek. He was visibly shaken.

'Aye, Bobby, son. You look like you're sickening for something. If I were you I'd see a doctor as soon as you set foot back in Manchester.' Shanks patted Bobby on the back and took off down the corridor, leaving him trembling in the foyer.

In the dressing room, Bobby was conspicuous by his absence and, ominously, there was a delay in announcing the team. We sat around kicking our heels, no one daring to get changed in case Matt Busby had a tactical plan which meant leaving one of us out. The thought of getting changed only to be told to put your clothes back on because you're not in the team is a player's nightmare.

Eventually Matt Busby entered the dressing room with Jimmy Murphy and told us they had reshuffled the team which had beaten West Ham the previous week. Bobby Charlton was unavailable. He'd suddenly been taken ill.

The following season we were back at Anfield and Shanks was up to his old tricks. As the United party made their way down the corridor to the away team changing room, he appeared from his office. 'Guess what, boys?' he said, brandishing a little orange ticket. 'I've had a go on the tickets that give the time when the away team will score. And it says here, in a fortnight!' With that, he disappeared back into his office.

We lost that encounter 2–0 and after the game I was chatting to Liverpool's Ray Clemence, who revealed to me another piece of Shankly kidology.

Prior to the game, Shankly had received the United team sheet and he incorporated it into his team talk. His intention was to run us down and, in so doing, boost the confidence of his own players. 'Alex Stepney,' Shanks began. 'A flapper of a goalkeeper. Hands like a Teflon frying pan – non-stick. Right back, Shay Brennan. Slow on the turn, give him a roasting.

Left back is Tony Dunne. Even slower than Brennan. He goes on an overlap at twenty past three and doesn't come back until a quarter to four. Right half, Nobby Stiles. A dirty little bastard. Kick him twice as hard as he kicks you and you'll have no trouble with him.'

'Bill Foulkes, a big, cumbersome centre half who can't direct his headers. He has a head like a sheriff's badge, so play on him. Paddy Crerand. Slower than steam rising off a dog turd. You'll bypass him easily.'

The Liverpool players felt as if they were growing in stature with his every word. 'David Sadler,' Shanks continued. 'Wouldn't get a place in our reserves. And finally, John Aston. A chicken, hit him once and you'll never hear from him again.' As the manager finished his demolition job on United, Emlyn Hughes raised his hand. 'That's all very well, boss,' he said, 'but you haven't mentioned George Best, Denis Law or Bobby Charlton.' Shanks turned on him. 'You mean to tell me we can't beat a team that has only three players in it?' he said, glowering.

32

Contract Time at the Cottage

I N the early sixties it was considered one of football's greatest
mysteries that Johnny Haynes, the highest-paid player in the
country and the England captain to boot, should be content to
spend his entire career with Fulham.

Fulham were destined to wander aimlessly up and down the
First Division ladder like a dog who had lost the scent. Usually
they'd end up contented in the lower half of the League but
safe from the jaws of relegation. Without doubt, Fulham could
never have been called a team of trophy-hunters.

Yet, while success and silverware may have been thin on
the ground, Fulham possessed more characters than a Chinese
typewriter. The club's chairman was Tommy Trinder, a radio
and TV comedian of great note who had learned his trade
in the variety halls and seemed to have brought along his
fellow performers from the end-of-pier playbills with him as
footballers and their agents, make-up artist and stage managers
as spectators.

In *Soccer Syndrome* (MacGibbon and Kee), written in the early
sixties, football writer John Moynihan summed up the whole
Fulham scene succinctly when he described it as 'a Saturday
afternoon team, offering a feeling of animated recreation
rather than solid professionalism ... a side of happy, sometimes comic triers watched by garrulous actors, serious actors,
pantomime players, band-leaders, stunt men, starlets; tweeds,

black leather, green leather, pink ankle-length knickers, baggy overcoats over armour-plated suede, cheroots between thumb and first finger'.

Amidst this cast from a Fellini film and a team who were at best 'happy triers' was England's most famous and adulated footballer of the time. Why? One can only assume that successive managers such as Bedford Jezzard, Vic Buckingham and Bill Dodgin had succeeded in selling Johnny Haynes a dream every time contracts were up for renewal. In the days when the only automatic sprinkler system for the pitch was the club cat and the only see-through thing a girl wore was her glasses, footballers were invited into the manager's office every two years and offered 'a deal'. If it was acceptable they simply signed on the dotted line, happy in the knowledge that come what may, they had an assured income for the next couple of years. A far cry from nowadays, when, more often than not, top players are not even present when new contracts are up for discussion and Gucci-suited agents do their talking for them.

Perhaps Johnny Haynes had been told that 'This year is going to be our year' and signed on the dotted line in the hope that it was. Alas for Fulham and Johnny, it never was their year. It was part of the manager's job to keep at the club the players who could ensure First Division survival, and Vic Buckingham did that by 'selling the dream'. Yet it was not without substance.

Fulham and Tommy Trinder in particular had a few bob. What was more, Tommy agreed to offer substantial bonuses to the players if they achieved success. According to those around the club at the time, Tommy had discovered a unique way of funding potential players' bonuses. Through a third party, he would put a large bet on Fulham to win the Cup, simply reach the final or win the League Championship. A number of different bets would also be placed on the club to finish second and third in the League. In the event that one of the bets came up, Tommy's winnings would be allocated amongst the players.

In short, the bonuses offered to the players were dependent on the odds Tommy's 'fixit' man could get from the bookies. The greater the odds, the bigger and better the bonuses would be. In part, it explains why some players might have been content to stay at Craven Cottage rather than trying their hand at a more fashionable club such as Arsenal or Chelsea. As the players used to say at the time, 'There's only one "F" in Fulham'.

Bobby Keetch played at full back or wing half in the sixties and was affectionately known by the Fulham faithful as Killer Keetch. Today Bobby is one of my best pals, though when I played against him, he showed precious little friendship towards me on the pitch.

Away from the ground, Bobby was a blond dandy in Italian patents and light slacks that stuck tighter to him than bark to a tree. A ladies' man, he was often to be seen in the passenger seat of some sports job driven by a blonde or brunette in headscarf and sunglasses. On the pitch he was the devil incarnate with a tackle like a sledgehammer. Come five o'clock on a Saturday, Vic Buckingham could never find him at the ground. 'Just left,' the manager would be told. 'Think he's gone into the boot room.'

'Left the boot room only a minute ago. Try the players' lounge.'

'Didn't you see him, gaffer? He must have passed you in the corridor, because he's just walked out of the room.'

The Pimpernel of Putney didn't hang around once his work on the field was over. He'd head for the Queen's Elm in Fulham Road for much-needed neck-oil before escorting a leggy female for the evening.

Bobby was called into Buckingham's office one hot June day. Youth team players lay in the centre of the overgrown pitch sunning themselves like cats whilst barebacked grounds staff leisurely slapped black paint on to the crush barriers, polka-dotting the terraces as they went along.

Bobby wore a short-sleeved shirt and slacks. Vic Buckingham, even though it was a hot, sticky day, wore his black Fulham blazer with its badge depicting crossed swords above an old sailing ship. Buckingham's once crisp white shirt was suffering from the heat and his black and white striped tie was attempting to escape from his top button. He indicated that Bobby was to be seated and produced two contracts from a drawer. He laid them on his desk, caressing each of their covers with the back of his hand as he did so.

'I've got two contracts here for you,' Buckingham told Bobby. 'Which one you choose is up to you.'

Bobby nodded to indicate he knew the score.

'This first one offers a basic weekly wage of forty pounds,' said Buckingham. 'Win, lose or draw, home or away, that's what you will get. There's nothing extra for winning away from home or finishing well up in the League. Do well in the Cups and you'll recieve not a penny more than that.'

Bobby let out a long sigh to show he was not impressed. 'And the other contract on offer?' he asked.

'The other contract contains bonuses that not even Spurs or Manchester United could offer you!' Buckingham said with great enthusiasm.

Bobby shuffled in his chair, taking a more upright position as his interest began to grow. 'Go on,' he said, urging his manager to reveal the jewels of the contract.

'It pays a basic wage of only twenty-five pounds a week,' Buckingham said. 'But it could make you a rich man, Bobby, son.'

Bobby's eyes lit up.

'For a start, if we finish in the top four of the League, you receive a thousand pounds. Win the League and you'll get two thousand!' Buckingham paused to let the facts sink in.

'What about win-and-draw bonus structure?' Bobby asked.

'Ten pounds extra for a home draw. Twenty pounds extra

for a home win. A thirty-pound bonus for an away draw and forty-quid bonus for an away win,' Buckingham said in a slow, assured voice.

Bobby's eyebrows went up. 'What about the Cups?' he asked, champing at the bit.

'Reach the FA Cup final and every player gets a thousand pounds. Win it and you get two thousand five hundred each.'

Bobby mopped the sweat from his brow with a crisp, linen handkerchief.

'Well?' Buckingham asked.

Bobby thought for a moment, then nodded to himself to confirm he was happy with the decision he had arrived at. 'I'll take the forty quid,' he said, extending a hand for contract and pen.

33

Billy Bingham

BILLY Bingham was the mercurial manager of Northern Ireland from 1977 to 1993. He had actually managed the national side prior to that, in a part-time capacity, whilst he was also manager of Everton.

Billy is a philosophical man, an impression underlined by the fact that he was often to be seen deep in thought whilst smoking contentedly on his pipe. Yet, for all his deep thinking, Billy could offer some true Irish gems. Before a game against West Germany he was without two or three key players due to injuries. 'Everything in our favour is against us today, lads!' he told us as he began his pre-match team talk.

Billy is a learned man, self-taught. During my Fulham days, I remember him boarding the team coach that was to take the Northern Ireland squad from our hotel to Windsor Park to a game against Iceland in 1978. Billy had spent most of his spare time at the hotel reading a book. He had carried on reading for the best part of the coach journey, but once put down his book when he left his seat to chat to some of the Northern Ireland officials.

Curious to find out what the book was, I jumped up and went to Billy's seat to look at the cover. When I returned, Jimmy Nichol, the Manchester United full back, asked me what the title was. 'The Diaries of James Joyce 1930 to 1935,' I told him.

A few minutes later, having absorbed the information, Jimmy

leaned across the aisle and tapped me on the shoulder. 'This Joyce must have been some kid,' he said, impressed. 'He kept a diary up to when he was five years old?'

When Billy took over full-time as Northern Ireland manager in 1977, his successor at Everton was a man named Gordon Lee. Lee joined Everton from Newcastle United, where he had enjoyed some success by taking them to a League Cup final at Wembley.

If a player is playing sufficiently well for his club, his manager will telephone the manager of the national side he is eligible to represent and recommend his inclusion in the squad. One day in 1980, Billy Bingham received a call from Gordon Lee about the Everton midfield player Eamon O'Keefe. 'I'm recommending him to you for the Northern Ireland squad,' Gordon told Billy.

'But he's not Irish,' Billy said.

'What do you mean, he's not Irish?' Gordon queried. 'His name is Eamon O'Keefe!'

'Yes, but he's not Irish,' repeated Billy. 'The lad was born in Manchester. He started out in non-league with Mossley.'

'Well, what business has anyone got naming him Eamon O'Keefe if he isn't Irish?' said Lee, somewhat miffed.

'Probably the same business they have naming you Lee when you're not Chinese!' said Billy.

34

My Pal Big Mal

MALCOLM ALLISON is a great pal. I love his dry sense of humour, his benign smile, his radical theories about football. There are few better ways to while away an afternoon than with a pot of tea, a big plate of sandwiches and Big Mal, as he puts forward his very personal theories on how the game of football should be played.

He started his playing career in the late 1940s with Charlton Athletic, who were managed at the time by Jimmy Seed. When National Service took him away from the Valley, Malcolm spent some time stationed in Austria with the army. He managed to get along to watch the likes of Rapid Vienna and Admira Wacker train and couldn't believe what he saw. The Austrians took their training and match preparation seriously. It was meticulously planned to get the most out of the players; it was varied, fun and the emphasis was on individual skills, where the ball was used at almost every opportunity.

This was in sharp contrast to what Malcolm knew from life at the Valley. At Charlton, Jimmy Seed hardly ever used the ball in training sessions, believing that if the players were denied the ball in training, it would make them all the more hungry to get it during a game on Saturday. As Malcolm told me once, there were a few players then at Charlton who, when they received the ball on a Saturday, hadn't a clue what to do with it!

Malcolm also noticed that the Austrian players were much

fitter and sharper than their British counterparts. Training at British clubs in the late forties and early fifties was far from the exact science it is today. The Charlton training consisted of a few laps around the cinder track that circled the pitch, followed by a little stretching of the limbs, then it was inside for a bath and a Woodbine.

When his National Service was over, Malcolm felt he had to speak up during his first training session back at the Valley. 'Can I make a point about the training, boss?' he asked Jimmy Seed.

'Sure,' said Seed.

'It's crap!'

A few weeks later Malcolm was called into Seed's office and told he was being transferred to West Ham. In five years at the Valley, Seed had only spoken directly to Malcolm on two occasions: the day he signed for Charlton and when he left for West Ham. 'I hope you have learned something from your time with me,' Seed said as Malcolm was leaving the manager's office.

'The art of communication,' replied Malcolm. 'You taught me how not to do it.'

'What makes you think you're so clever?' Seed asked bitterly.

'Talking to you,' said Malcolm as he closed the door behind him.

Malcolm flourished at what was called the 'West Ham academy' under manager Ted Fenton and his assistant, Ron Greenwood, who would himself go on to manage the club for thirteen years before accepting the post as England manager.

I've always believed that a team is an extension of its manager. Managers usually sign players who play the game the way they like to see it played. This was the case when Malcom was at West Ham. It was a breeding ground for those who believed football should be played openly and entertainingly and who would carry that gospel into management themselves.

His team-mates included Ken Brown, who was later to have considerable success as manager of Norwich City, John Bond, whose managerial career took in Norwich, Manchester City, Birmingham City, Bournemouth and Shrewsbury Town, and Noel Cantwell, a former team-mate of mine who later managed Peterborough United. Towards the end of Malcolm's playing days, West Ham introduced a batch of youngsters whom Malcolm knew had the class and style to make a big impression at the very top. They included Bobby Moore, Geoff Hurst and Martin Peters.

Malcolm tells me that one day, the youngsters from the West Ham academy, including the likes of Moore and Hurst, had been sent on a long cross-country run whilst the senior players such as himself trained at the training ground. When the youngsters returned Malcolm asked Ron Greenwood if he thought the young lads were honest and trustworthy.

'Very honest,' Greenwood replied.

'Then why do you accompany them on a bike every inch of the way when they go off on a long-distance run?' asked Malcolm.

'To keep them honest!' Greenwood replied.

Life at West Ham was much more to Malcolm's liking than at Charlton. The training was more varied and interesting and the players much more mentally attuned to the game. The care and intelligence that went into training and matches also manifested itself when the players were relaxing and occupying themselves.

On long away trips, the players would often pass the time with games that involved some degree of mental agility. On one occasion, during a trip north to play Sheffield United, the players had gathered around the back seat of their team coach for a game which involved making up a story. Each player had to make up a sentence which included a word chosen by the previous player. The idea was that each sentence had to make sense and follow on from the previous one so that the story would develop.

'Overcoat!' John Bond said to Malcolm, whose turn it was next.'

'I bought a new overcoat and I think it's great,' said Malcolm as he turned to the player next to him, centre half John Dicks. 'Fascinate!' said Malcolm to the big, brawny centre half.

Dicks thought it over for twenty seconds or so whilst the rest of the players urged him to hurry up. Eventually Dicks excitedly drew himself up in his seat: 'I bought a new overcoat and I think it's great,' he said. 'It's got nine buttons but I can only fascinate!'

Brawny centre halves apart, Malcolm benefited greatly from his 'education' at Upton Park. Along with his own innovative ideas, it was to launch him on a highly successful managerial career. It began in the non-league game with Bath City then progressed to Manchester City, where, as assistant to the late Joe Mercer and later manager himself, he enjoyed considerable success. Some of Malcolm's ideas may have been controversial, such as appointing a psychiatrist to study players' mental attitudes, but City achieved unprecedented success the Allison way.

They won the Second Division in 1966 and followed it by winning the First Division Championship in 1968, the FA Cup in 1969 and the League Cup and the European Cup-Winners' Cup in 1970. In the Cup-Winners' Cup final, goals from two of the most ardent devotees of the Allison style, Neil Young and Francis Lee, saw City beat Polish side Gornik Zabrze in, of all places, Vienna. Malcolm had not forgotten the lessons he learned in his formative days in Austria.

In 1980, Malcolm took over from Ernie Whalley as manager of Crystal Palace. It was, in fact, his second spell as manager at Selhurst Park – he been there from 1973 to 1976, when he took the team and his famous fedora hat to the FA Cup semi-finals. Malcolm was filled with optimism about that second spell at Palace. I can remember him telling me he was developing what he considered to be the best group of young players he had ever handled. They were, he told me, going to be 'the team of the eighties'. Malcolm also told the media, and when the team failed to live up to his expectations and were relegated to Division Two, the press, as is their wont, threw his words back in his face with a vengeance.

It was this team which produced my favourite story about Malcolm. It centred on the fact that his Palace team was made up of a roughly equal number of black and white players. Malcolm had invited me to travel with Palace to an away fixture at Old Trafford. The team were to travel by coach on the Friday and stay over for the game on Saturday. Malcolm had arranged for the two of us to meet one of his former players, Mike Summerbee, for a meal in Manchester on the Friday night. On arriving at Selhurst Park, I was surprised to find the team coach empty although there were only five minutes to go before departure.

On entering the offices I met Malcolm, who told me he had taken the players off the coach as there was a problem brewing and he wanted to nip it in the bud. I followed him to the home-team dressing room where all the players were seated. The black guys were on one side of the room, the white lads on the other.

'Right,' Malcolm began authoritatively. 'It has been brought to my notice that we may have a silly problem brewing here. That we might have a "black and white" thing at the club.'

The players sat in silence staring at the floor.

'When I ask you to form yourself into teams in training, I invariably end up with one team of black players and one of white players. Worse still, I've heard you goading one another after games. If we win, you black lads say it is down to you.

You white guys say it is you lot who won it for us. When we lose, you blame each other.'

Malcolm heaved his considerable chest as he took a great intake of breath and proceeded to lay down the law. 'It stops, and it stops this minute!' he said menacingly. 'I will not have a black versus white, or white versus black thing at this club! We are all individuals and we are a team. We play together as one. Anyone who doesn't like that idea can bugger off now. Do you understand?'

The Palace players nodded sheepishly.

'From now on, as far as I'm concerned,' Malcolm continued, 'there are no black players and there are no white players. From now on, you're all green.'

The players looked up in surprise.

'All green, OK?' Malcolm reiterated looking for agreement.

The players nodded.

'OK, that's it then. Now let's have you on that coach to Manchester. Dark greens at the front, light greens at the back!'

35

Frank Words

THE year 1972 was not a happy one for me. Matt Busby had retired and gone 'upstairs' to the boardroom. His replacement, the affable and staunch United loyalist, Wilf McGuinness, lasted just a year before he too was replaced, by Frank O'Farrell. Poor Wilf. If anyone had been a tremendous servant to Manchester United it was he.

Wilf had joined United straight from school in 1954. He was playing first-team football at seventeen and for England at nineteen. At the age of twenty-two he sustained a stress fracture of the leg. Complications set in and, reserve games apart, he was never to play for United again. He was appointed coach to the United youth team and over the years progressed through the managerial ranks to become first-team coach. When Matt Busby decided to call it a day in 1969, Wilf's wildest dream came true. He was appointed manager.

Wilf inherited an ageing side. He knew star players such as Bobby Charlton, Denis Law and Paddy Crerand had to be replaced; his dilemma was, by whom? How can you go out and find another Bobby Charlton or Denis Law? Wilf knew what had to be done and had the courage of his convictions but he had not been in the managerial hot seat long when he caused an uproar by dropping both Bobby and Denis.

The board wanted immediate success and that meant the First Division Championship. Wilf was unable to repeat the success of 1967 and after eighteen years at Old Trafford, as man and boy, he was called to see Matt Busby in the boardroom.

'Wilf,' Matt said gravely. 'You've been at this club since you were a small boy. For over eighteen years, you've given this club your all and I don't know how we could get by without you. But we're going to give it a try.'

That was it. Wilf was gone.

What people do not know is that Wilf had not been allowed to sign young players he saw as ideal replacements for those getting on in years. He had gone to the board with the names of three players he wanted to buy. The board, however, didn't rate them as highly as Wilf did and he was refused the money. The careers of Malcolm Macdonald, Mick Mills and Colin Todd were to develop elsewhere at the highest level.

At the time, Wilf was totally devastated by his sacking. It affected him so badly he lost all his hair – more or less overnight. I see him regularly nowadays on the after-dinner speaking circuit and only recently asked him if he was still bitter about the way he was dispensed with at United, and whether it preyed on his mind to this day.

'Of course not!' Wilf said emphatically. 'A lot of time has passed since then. After all, it is twenty-two years' – he looked at his watch – 'three months, two days, one hour and twenty-four minutes since it happened!'

Whilst Wilf was an outgoing man with a ready wit, his replacement, Frank O'Farrell, was a dour and serious individual. Frank had enjoyed considerable success in the lower divisions with Torquay United and had taken Leicester City to the Cup final in 1969, but as a manager he had never won any of the game's honours.

Wilf had been refused money to buy the likes of Macdonald, Todd and Mills, but Frank was given the funds to enter the transfer market. He bought Wyn Davies, a giant of a centre forward who was so tall I used to think he must have fallen asleep in a greenhouse when he was a kid. The trouble was, Wyn's days as a kid had long since passed. He was as old as the players Frank was looking to replace.

Ian Storey-Moore came from Nottingham Forest. The winger was not without ability but he was terribly injury-prone. He was the only player I ever saw strain a calf muscle whilst putting on a sock. He spent most of his time at United in the treatment room and was never fit enough to make a real contribution. Ian suffered for it by never becoming popular with the Old Trafford fans. In one game at home to Everton he received the ball out on the touchline. He waved his right foot over the ball as if placing it under his spell and looked ready to dance his way down the wing leaving a trail of defenders in his wake. Suddenly a voice called from the paddock terrace.

'Give us some magic, Ian!'

Quick as a flash, another voice came back. 'Aye, do us all a favour and bloody disappear!'

Ian put his foot on the ball, stumbled and the ball squirmed away from him for an Everton throw-in.

'Moore, you're about as useful as a back pocket in a vest!' the first voice boomed out.

That sort of barracking had been unheard of in previous years at Old Trafford. But it started to become a regular thing and it spoke volumes about the quality of player that was being brought into the club.

I started to become very disillusioned. In hindsight, I should have asked for a transfer as I'm sure the fresh challenge would have done me good. There was talk of me moving to Chelsea, but nothing came of it. My motivation and application dipped and I started to go absent without leave.

When I did play it was heartbreaking. I've played in charity games where stars from other sports or TV personalities give up their time to raise money for a worthy cause. Many haven't a clue how to play football, so in such games you avoid passing the ball to them as you know the move will break down. It was like that playing for United under Frank O'Farrell. There were United players to whom I would consciously avoid giving the ball, as I knew nothing productive would come of it.

Frank's only signing to make a positive contribution to the club was Martin Buchan, who joined us from Aberdeen. He was a stylish centre back who continued his educational studies during his spell with United and eventually became a languages graduate. I think everyone admired Martin for the way he combined a playing career with his studies, but it did give rise to some gentle ribbing.

I remember I used to have a long, navy blue overcoat I occasionally wore when the weather was bad. I boarded the coach to an away game one January day and Martin remarked how much he liked the coat. 'From its style, it looks French,' he said.

'It is from France,' I told him. 'It's Toulon and Toulouse!'

During 1971–72 results under Frank got worse and for me it all culminated in an away game at Elland Road. Leeds were locked in a three-horse race for the championship with Liverpool and the eventual winners, Derby County. Elland Road had become a fortress and not many sides came away from there with a draw, never mind a win. Just about every player in their side was an international and it included the likes of David Harvey, Billy Bremner, Paul Madeley, Eddie Gray and Peter Lorimer. We had a number of injuries and even by the standards at that time it was a weakened side we put out to face Leeds.

The buzzer sounded in the changing room and we rose to our feet, forming a crocodile line as we prepared to take the pitch. A deafening roar shook the room as 45,000 Leeds fans welcomed their team on to the field.

I turned to Frank O'Farrell, who was standing in the middle

of the room. He was not the best communicator and had said nothing to raise our hopes and confidence. 'Boss?' I said, nodding towards him in an effort to get him to offer some support and encouragement as we prepared to take on Leeds.

Frank gave me a puzzled look, not knowing what I wanted him to do.

'Come on, boss,' I said clenching my fist and nodding back along the line of players to indicate I wanted him to say a few words of encouragement.

He raised his eyebrows and the first finger of his right hand as it dawned on him that I wanted him to say something.

'Ah, yes!' he said as he searched his mind for the right phrase. We all turned and looked back to hear our leader's morale-lifting words.

'Cheerio, boys!' he said brightly as we filed out of the door on our way to another defeat.

Directors

'What this club needs is a manager who can get it right and be our manager at the same time.'

Keith Collins, former Sunderland chairman.

'If you build a big successful business from a football club, you're a sinister influence. If you don't, you're a bloody failure.'

Tommy Trinder, former Fulham chairman.

36

Chairmen and Directors

L EN SHACKLETON, who played for Bradford, Newcastle, Sunderland and Arsenal in the 1940s and 1950s, said it all. He was known as the Clown Prince of Soccer and in his autobiography he devoted a three-page chapter to what football club directors know about football: all three pages were blank.

Not all directors are meddlesome. Some, like John Smith, the former chairman of Liverpool, and his co-directors, had the wisdom to stay out of the manager's way and let him get on with the job of managing the club. They allowed Bill Shankly and his successors, Bob Paisley and Joe Fagan, to manage without interference and Liverpool enjoyed unrivalled success in the sixties, seventies and eighties. Three decades brought fifteen League Championships, four FA Cup triumphs, four League Cups, four European Cup and two UEFA Cup victories.

For seventeen years Brian Clough had no interference from his board and brought great success to Nottingham Forest. Further down the League ladder, Dario Gradi has since 1983 been allowed to put his ideas of grooming young players into practice at Crewe Alexandra. Before Dario was appointed, Crewe were a club forever floundering at the basement of the Football League. In recent years, Dario has produced David Platt, who went to Aston Villa and subsequently Sampdoria, and, of course, became England captain, Craig Hignett, who Middlesbrough purchased for £750,000 in 1992, Rob Jones, who joined Liverpool for £500,000, and a host of other players who have joined clubs in the higher echelons of the League for big transfer fees. Dario coached them, nurtured them, sold them on for handsome profits and still had players of sufficient quality to win promotion to Division 2 in 1994.

Other managers are not so lucky. When my friend John McGrath, the former Newcastle and Southampton centre half, was appointed manager of Halifax Town in 1991, he was their twenty-third manager since 1945 and their seventh in ten years. He tells me it wasn't the fact that his name was written on the door of the manager's office in chalk that made him feel uneasy – it was the sponge on the string hanging from the outside door handle! On his first day as manager at Halifax Town, one of the club's directors called into John's office to introduce himself. After wishing John good luck he said, 'The thing about being a football manager is that every day that dawns is one day nearer to the day you get the sack!'

When Tommy Docherty went to manage Second Division Rotherham United in 1967, it was a club on the slide with a run-down ground. Soon after his appointment, Tommy was being shown around the ground by the Rotherham chairman when they came across a ramshackle wooden hut at the side of the main stand.

'What a bloody eyesore,' Tommy said, pointing to the old hut. 'This old shack will have to go for a start.'

'This is your office!' the chairman told Tommy defensively.

Wilf McGuinness went on to manage York City between 1975 and 1977. He managed York in the Fourth, Third and Second Divisions in successive seasons – unfortunately, in reverse order. Wilf realised his days as manager were numbered when he was sitting next to the York chairman, Mr Sinclair, at a sportsman's dinner in a York hotel one wet

and windy night in March. Halfway through the meal, the hotel manager approached Sinclair.

'Mr Sinclair, I think you should inform your fellow diners that the heavy rain has caused the River Ouse to overflow its banks,' he said with an air of concern. 'It's tragic. The water is coming this way and we could be in for a disaster.'

'What would be tragic would be Wilf McGuinness falling into the river,' Sinclair said. 'And the disaster would be if he didn't drown!'

Wilf decided against viewing the house he and his wife Beryl were considering buying in York.

When I went to play for Fulham in 1977, the chairman, Ernie Clay, offered Rodney Marsh and me contracts whereby we earned very lucrative bonuses every time the team won and an extra bonus for each goal Rodney and I scored. The team started doing very well, with Rodney and I scoring lots of goals. After six weeks, whenever Rodney or I got anywhere near the opponents' penalty area with the ball, Ernie would jump up in the directors' box and scream to the linesman, 'Offside!'

In the sixties and seventies Rochdale were always strapped for cash. Clubs at that time were not geared to the commercial side of football as they are today. The gate money received by clubs like Rochdale was nowhere near enough to survive on, so they had to conjure up funds from any and every source.

In the mid-seventies, the Rochdale chairman was a man named Denis Wrigley. He had a friend who owned racehorses and, after much badgering and pleading, Wrigley persuaded his friend to donate one of his horses to Rochdale so that it could be raffled amongst the town's local business people to raise funds for the club.

Wrigley and his fellow directors priced the tickets at £50 each, which, considering the prize was a thoroughbred racehorse, was very reasonable, even in the seventies. For weeks they sold them around local businesses in the Rochdale area, but, on the day before the raffle was to be drawn, Wrigley received a call from the club secretary, Mrs Rawlinson, telling him the tragic news that the horse had died of a heart attack.

A week or so later, Wrigley's racing friend who had donated the horse rang him up. 'Sorry to hear about the horse,' the owner said. 'Terrible bad luck and a great pity, because it would have raised a lot of money for your club.'

'Oh, it raised well into four figures,' Wrigley said. 'One of the best fund-raisers we've ever had!'

'You raffled a dead horse and got no complaints?' his friend asked, puzzled.

'Only the one complaint,' said Wrigley. 'From the guy who won the raffle. So I gave him his fifty pounds back.'

Mike Summerbee has been a good friend of mine since the sixties. I got to know him when he played for Manchester City and he tells me some amazing stories about life at Maine Road when Joe Mercer and Malcolm Allison were in charge between 1965 and 1972. The City chairman was a man called Albert Alexander, who was a Christian Scientist and totally against gambling, smoking and drinking. As for the other unmentionable, it was for procreation only.

After a City–United derby in 1969, I was chatting with Malcolm Allison when Albert came up to him. 'I just want you to know that as your chairman I'm right behind you,' Albert said to Malcolm.

'I'd prefer it if you were in front of me,' Malcolm replied, 'so I can see what you're up to!'

For years City had gone without success, but under Joe Mercer and Malcolm the good times started to return to Maine Road. In 1969, Manchester City met Everton in an FA Cup semi-final at Villa Park. It was a tense affair – the teams were well matched and went at one another tooth and nail. With a minute remaining and the score at 0–0, City won a corner. From it, centre back Tommy Booth scored the only goal of the game. Manchester City were at Wembley in an FA Cup final for the first time since 1956.

The dressing room after the game was like a battlefield. The players sat, there, elated but exhausted. It had been a tough, physical game. Mike Summerbee had a wound to his right knee which required nine stitches. Colin Bell, who had played magnificently in midfield, was not letting the broken nose he had picked up in the game spoil his enjoyment of victory. Full back Glyn Pardoe and centre back Mike Doyle had both picked up bad injuries, but they had played through the pain barrier rather than leave the field. Both were laid out on the dressing-room floor receiving treatment when Malcolm Allison called for quiet. Albert Alexander had entered the room. 'Let's have your attention, lads,' Malcolm shouted. 'Your chairman wants to say a few words to you all.'

'Well done, lads,' Albert told the exhausted team. 'We're in an FA Cup final at Wembley for the first time in thirteen years. That's great, because it will generate the money we need to buy some decent players instead of you lot!'

37

Oh, Lord!

A s I said earlier, there was a period from 1966 to 1969 when
I found it difficult to walk down the street without being
besieged by people wanting a chat or an autograph. I understood
that I would have to accept it, but on occasions it got silly. I
remember leaving my home in Bramall one Sunday morning at
about 11:30 to walk the quarter of a mile or so to the local
newsagent to buy a Sunday paper. By the time I reached the
shop, I had an entourage of around thirty people following
me. The newsagent had one of the biggest disappointments
of his life – all those people in his shop and he only sold one
Sunday Mirror.

It reached the stage where I didn't enjoy going out. I would
on occasions, though, borrow the car that belonged to my mate,
the singer and actor Kenny Lynch, and just go out and drive. I
had an E-Type Jaguar at the time, and I thought Kenny's Ford
Cortina would be less conspicuous. Having borrowed Kenny's
car one Sunday morning in 1968, I drove north of Manchester
and found myself coasting around the streets of Burnley.

I used to get a buzz on such trips by thinking, 'Here I am,
Britain's most sought-after footballer, driving around Burnley
on a Sunday morning. If the press wanted to find me, they
never could.'

I realised I was passing Turf Moor, the home of Burnley FC.
The area around the ground was a maze of terraced houses,

back to back, with the odd patch of waste ground where some had been demolished. Being a Sunday morning it was quiet – a quiet that for me was all the more pronounced because the only time I had ever seen Turf Moor and its immediate vicinity was when United played there and the streets were thronged with supporters.

I stopped the car and got out. A group of young boys were kicking a plastic ball around a stretch of ground where houses had once stood. Feeling there was sufficient distance between us, I decided to watch them.

They played as all small boys do: shouting and screaming instructions in shrill voices and theatrically flinging themselves around the mud and asphalt as if they believed that the dirtier they became, the better they had performed. Flushed and animated, the boys whooped every time a goal was scored.

'I'm Frank Casper,' one called out, assuming the identity of the current Burnley centre forward.

'Thou's not,' shouted another, much larger, lad. 'I baggsied being Casper, thou's Mick Docherty!'

The smaller boy thought for a moment. 'Aye, alreet. Doch'tee will do,' the smaller boy said, and immediately resumed playing, happy in the knowledge that he was someone. When the boys fell, they'd scramble back to their feet again, giving only a cursory look at grazed knees. They gave one another a vigorous buffeting but needed no referee to run the game. When someone was fouled, they had a free kick. When a goal was scored between the pile of coats that acted as posts, the ball was returned to the centre of the waste ground for the game to restart with a kick-off. They knew the rules and played to them.

I was about to get into the car when I suddenly noticed someone standing next to me. 'They're our future,' a thick Lancastrian accent said. 'Amidst all this debris of t' past. Yon lads are t' future.'

My peace and solitude broken, I wanted to beat a hasty

retreat back to the car and drive away, but the voice spoke again.

'They want to be Frank Casper or Mick Docherty, because for an hour or so, it helps them escape from all this.'

I turned and saw that the man was pointing to the rows of terraced houses all around us. He was thick-set, in his late seventies and about five feet ten tall. His dark hair was flattened with brilliantine and grey at the temples. His face looked dour and solemn and the bags under his eyes gave him a permanently soured expression. His overcoat was light tweed and expensive. Underneath he wore a navy blue three-piece suit with a watch and chain that even in 1968 was an anachronism. I recognised him immediately. He was Bob Lord, the Chairman of Burnley.

In my old jumper and jeans the old guy hadn't recognised me. I wasn't surprised: he was probably used to seeing me in the United strip and even then at some distance. Then again, who would expect to see George Best hanging around the streets of Burnley at 10.30 on a Sunday morning?

'I escaped from here,' Lord said, gazing around. 'Built up a butchery business. Done alreet an' all. Got mesel' big house up by Padiham. Can see River Calder on one side, an't' Forest of Pendle ont tuther.'

'Sounds nice. You obviously don't recog – '

Lord waved his right hand at me and cut me short. 'Save thee breath, lad. Haven't got me hearing aid in. Can't hear a thing, deaf as a post wirrout.'

I nodded. We gazed around for a few seconds, then Lord sighed softly. 'Funny thing is, now that I've got the big house, the money, al't' bloody pressure of business an't' like, I come back 'ere. I got what I always wanted in life, now I feel t' need to escape. That's why I'm 'ere, ten-thirty ont Sunday mornin', when there's nobody t' bother me. I can be meself for't change.'

I smiled, slightly embarrassed, as I stooped to get back into the car.

'Think on what I've said, lad,' Lord said as he turned to walk towards Turf Moor.

'Stupid old sod,' I muttered as I shut the car door and started the engine.

On the way back to Bramall, I thought about what Bob Lord had said. The more I thought about it in relation to my own life, the more profound I thought it was. I realised the need to escape occasionally was essential. Whether to a football match on a Saturday afternoon, a visit to the pictures, or whatever. We all need to escape from something and discover our true selves.

Later that season, when United entertained Burnley at Old Trafford, I was determined to seek out Bob Lord and ask him if he remembered talking to a shaggy-haired young man wearing an old sweater and jeans one Sunday morning near Burnley's ground.

I managed to find him coming out of the Old Trafford director's Lounge. I recalled the Sunday morning he had planted the seeds in my mind which had taught me something about life.

'It was me,' I told him. 'Only you didn't recognise me.'

'Course I knew it were you!' Lord said. 'Only I reckoned you were doing your own bit of escaping, so I pretended I didn't know who thee were.'

I thanked him and said that this time I was glad he was wearing his hearing aid so we could chat. As we parted he turned to me. 'An' another thing, George, lad,' he said, an impish smile breaking through the dour expression. 'Don't call someone who's trying to give thee some fatherly advice a "stupid old sod"!'

38

Tommy Trinder

TOMMY TRINDER was the charismatic chairman of Fulham in the fifties and sixties. Tommy was a comedian who had come up the hard way through the variety halls and adapted to radio and film as well as the emerging medium of television with seemingly little effort. A football fanatic and lifelong devotee of Fulham, he was a great character whose protruding chin, camel-hair coat and trilby hat were as synonymous with Fulham as the cottage in the corner of the ground itself.

Following a game against Fulham at Craven Cottage in 1964, I was having a drink in the players' lounge as Tommy, his fellow directors and their wives entertained their United counterparts in the same room. At the time, Fulham had a groundsman called Reg Barrow, who, if appropriately dressed, was allowed to socialise with the directors and their wives after the game.

Reg was in conversation with the wife of our chairman, Louis Edwards. Mrs Edwards, a very prim and proper lady, asked Reg what his role at Fulham was and on being told that he was the head groundsman, she remarked on how good the Fulham pitch was looking so late in the season: 'It still has plenty of grass on it. Remarkable considering there must be two or three games a week played on it.'

'It's all the manure I put on it in the close season,' Reg said proudly. 'Barrowload after barrowload of stinking, steaming manure, that's the secret.'

Having been put off her plate of cucumber sandwiches, Mrs Edwards excused herself and made her way to where her husband Louis was in conversation with Tommy Trinder. Tommy asked Mrs Edwards if she was enjoying her visit to Fulham and was somewhat taken aback when she told him she was, but could he do something about the language of his head groundsman?

'Can you talk him into using the word "fertiliser", when he refers to what he has to put on your pitch?' said Mrs Edwards. 'He uses the word "manure", and I find it so distasteful.'

'Blimey!' said Tommy, grinning from ear to ear. 'I don't think I'd be able to get Reg to say "fertiliser". It took me six months to get him to call it manure!'

Tommy was a lovable character, larger than life, who was always ready with a quip or funny remark. He told me it often enabled him to get out of a sticky mess, such as the time he was a guest of Portsmouth in 1956.

Tommy was appearing in a seaside show at Southsea when he received an invitation from the president of Portsmouth, Field-Marshall the Viscount Montgomery of Alamein, KG, GCB, DSO – the man who had led the British Desert Rats to victory over Rommel in North Africa during World War Two – to attend a Portsmouth home game as his guest. Tommy was delighted. After the game, Tommy was in the Portsmouth boardroom listening to the results of all the other games that afternoon on the radio, keeping a keen ear open for any news of Fulham.

Finally, the radio presenter announced that Fulham had beaten Sheffield Wednesday 2–0, and that both goals had been scored by Johnny Haynes. 'He's going to be a great player,' said Tommy, glowing with pride. 'Mark my words, Viscount, Haynes will play for England one day. Another two goals today! He's a brilliant player, and only eighteen years of age.'

'Eighteen years old?' said Viscount Montgomery sternly, dampening Tommy's ardour. 'Why the hell isn't he doing his National Service?'

'Well, that's the only sad thing about him,' Tommy said, quick as a flash, taking a long draw on his cigar. 'He's a cripple!'

Tosh Chamberlain was a good winger who was as eccentric as a dotty aunt but a big favourite with the Fulham fans. I remember, during my first visit to Craven Cottage, Tony Dunne dumping Tosh on the ground and the referee waving play on as he saw nothing wrong with the sledgehammer tackle.

Tosh, livid at being on the receiving end of what he believed to be a bad tackle that had gone unpunished, simply sat cross-legged on the ground for a full two minutes as the game buzzed on around him. Eventually, when the ball went out of play for a throw-in to United, the referee marched across to Tosh and demanded he stood up.

'Not until you bleedin' well apologise for that terrible decision!' Tosh told him.

Tosh's reputation as a character was legendary amongst players, but he outdid himself one Saturday in 1965. Fulham had been the visitors to Old Trafford and Tommy Trinder and a young Fulham reserve player called Rodney Marsh, who had not played against us but had made the journey as a squad member, were chatting to me over a drink.

United had won the game 2–0 and I remarked that I felt we could have won by more but for some fine saves from the Fulham goalkeeper, John McClelland, who was deputising for their regular first-team keeper, Tony Macedo. Tommy and Rodney agreed that McCelland had turned in an inspired performance in stepping up to the first team. 'I take it Tony Macedo is injured, then?' I asked.

'Oh, haven't you boys up north heard?' said Tommy.

'Heard what?'

'About Macedo. He broke his ribs last Saturday against Leeds. Only it wasn't a Leeds player what done it. It was one of ours, Tosh Chamberlain!'

Tommy and Rodney went on to tell me how, on the previous Saturday, at the beginning of the second half, Tosh had come back to help his defence cope with an onslaught from visitors Leeds. In the opening minutes of the half, the Fulham penalty box was packed with players following a corner which Fulham managed to clear. As both sets of players streamed out of the penalty box, the Leeds full back, Paul Reaney, latched on to the ball and lobbed it over everyone's heads.

The ball landed on the edge of the Fulham penalty area, half way between goalkeeper Tony Macedo and the rest of the players. Tosh Chamberlain was the first to react. He turned and sprinted back towards the bouncing ball as Macedo ran towards it from his goal-line. With both goalkeeper and Tosh an equal distance from the ball, it was a toss-up who would reach it first. Tosh's speed as a winger won the day and he reached the still bouncing ball just a few paces before Macedo. Now, normally in such a situation, one of two things would happen. The player would either, with a deft touch of the foot, gently lift it the two yards into the goalkeeper's hands; or, turn sideways on to the advancing goalkeeper and hit the ball with such venom that it would go over the top of the stand like a missile and off into orbit around the world.

But, as Tommy pointed out to me, Tosh was far from your 'normal' player. On reaching the ball, Tosh bent his head forward, jumped a foot off the ground and, mustering all his weight and strength into one combined effort, blasted the ball into the midriff of the advancing Macedo, who by then was only three feet away.

Macedo hit the ground like a sack of potatoes, three ribs broken, unable to breathe as the air left his body in one cannonball rush.

As the trainers and St John's Ambulance attendants raced on to the pitch, Fulham's Bobby Keetch was first on the scene. 'You stupid, soppin' bastard!' Keetch raged at Tosh. 'What did you wanna go and do that for?'

Tosh stood bemused, arms out wide, the palms of his hands turned upwards. 'I just looked up and saw the goal,' he pleaded. 'For a split second, me head went and I thought I'd have a go. I forgot we'd changed ends at half-time!'

My favourite story concerning Tommy Trinder happened at a game between England Under-23s and their Northern Ireland counterparts, for whom I was playing. The match took place in 1963 at Upton Park, the home of West Ham, and Tommy had come along especially to watch the Fulham right back, George Cohen. Each team was allowed one over-age player and George had been included in the England line-up as Alf Ramsey was thinking of bringing him into the full international side in place of Blackpool's Jimmy Armfield. As it happened, George had a super game and went on to play for the full England team and later star in their World Cup success of 1966.

Following the game, which England won 4–1, George Cohen, my Irish team-mate Martin Harvey and myself were enjoying some good-humoured mickey-taking in the players' bar when Tommy joined us.

'So when you have children, what will you put your boy to?' George Cohen asked Martin.

'Well, I'd like him to enter the Church and lead a life free from sin,' said Martin in all seriousness.

'That's no life for a boy. He wouldn't thank you for that,' George said.

'You never know, he might rise through the ranks and become a bishop,' Martin reasoned.

'And spend his life living on charity?' said George disapprovingly.

'He might even become the Pope!' said Martin, sticking to his point.

'And be locked away in the Vatican and never see anything of the world?' George said. 'Not much of a life.'

Martin, getting a little vexed, slammed his drink down on the table. 'And just what would you want the boy to be?' he asked, angered. 'The Lord Jesus Christ Himself?'

Tommy, sensing the conversation was getting over-heated, intervened by throwing his arm around George Cohen and offering one of his big, wide grins. 'Well, why not?' he said, pointing at George Cohen. 'One of his boys made it!'

The Games

'It was a ginger ale sort of game. It fizzed like mad for ten minutes then went flat.'

Malcolm Allison, former Manchester City manager.

'I drank twenty cups of coffee during that game. It still didn't keep me awake.'

Terry Venables, former Queen's Park Rangers manager.

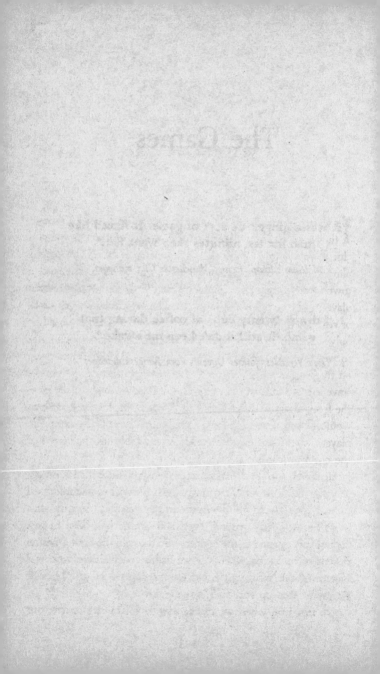

39

Forest Away

I F I were to ask any of today's players to direct me to a ground they have recently played at, my guess is they wouldn't have a clue where to start. Footballers are notorious for not taking the blindest bit of notice where they are going when they visit a town or city for an away game. I was no different. When United played away I would while away the coach journey playing cards or reading. If I looked out of the window at all, then it would be only a cursory glance. It was 1964–65, the season in which I was to win my first League Championship medal, and United were on the way to a League game at Nottingham Forest. When we travelled to away games by coach Matt Busby would usually sit at the front along with his assistant, Jimmy Murphy. Behind them would be our secretary, Les Olive, and a knot of directors. We players would scatter ourselves from the tables in the centre of the coach towards the back seat.

However, on this particular day, Matt Busby and Jimmy Murphy didn't travel to Nottingham with us. They had informed us that they would go independently by car and meet up with us at Forest's City ground. Matt and Jimmy had been to just about every ground in the country and those in the First Division dozens of times. So whenever we had a coach driver who was unsure of the way, you could always depend on the boss or Jimmy to step up and offer directions.

On this trip, when we reached Nottingham city centre, our

coach pulled over to the roadside. Engine idling, our driver turned and asked if anyone knew the way out of the centre to the City ground. At first there was silence. Everyone looked at one another with bemused faces.

'Forest's ground, Notts County's ground and the Trent Bridge cricket ground are all near one another. They're almost on the same road,' Bobby Charlton ventured.

Heads nodded in agreement.

'Right, but how do I get out to them?' the driver asked.

Again there was silence for a moment.

'I've played here a few times,' said Denis Law. 'I think you want to follow this road out of the city, then turn left.'

'That'll take us back to Derby,' Alex Stepney said. 'We don't want that!'

'In that case, I think we should turn right at the end of this road,' I said, throwing in my two penn'orth.

'We made that mistake two years ago and got lost,' said Bill Foulkes. 'We don't want to be going right, George.'

The debate continued and the Nottingham traffic built up behind us as it slowly circumnavigated our stationary bus.

Eventually, our captain, Paddy Crerand, jumped to his feet. 'Here's a policeman,' he said, pointing to a young constable. 'I'll nip out and get directions.'

After about five minutes, Denis Law and I began to wonder what was taking Paddy so long. Surely it wouldn't take five minutes to get a simple set of instructions? One or two of the players, myself included, started to knock on the coach window to indicate that Paddy should get a move on. But he went on chatting away with this fresh-faced young policeman.

After ten minutes, we started to whistle and goad Paddy. If we didn't get a move on, we'd arrive at the City ground late. Worse still, if we were so late that the boss could not hand in our teamsheet before the 2.15 deadline, the club would incur a hefty fine, and then there would be all hell to pay.

At first Paddy tried to hush us with a dismissive wave of his arm, but as the appeals for him to hurry got louder, he came back up the steps of the coach and stood by the driver. 'Listen, just be patient will you? This young fella is from Mansfield. He's only a special constable and it's his first day on duty in Nottingham. Paddy's voice had a note of sympathy. He doesn't know the way to Forest's ground, but the bobby he's been assigned to for the afternoon should be here any minute.'

The catcalling had died down as Paddy spoke. For a moment nobody spoke. Then Denis Law piped up.

'A policeman and he doesn't know the way to Nottingham Forest's ground?' he shouted. 'No bloody wonder they never caught Robin Hood!'

40

Chester in the Cup

I N 1965 Manchester United were drawn at home to Chester City in the third round of the FA Cup. It seemed a formality that we would progress into the fourth round as we had home advantage and Chester were in the lower reaches of Division Four at the time. As it happened, though, Chester proved stubborn opposition and United scraped home 2–1.

The 1964–65 season was a difficult one for me as I was dogged by an injury to my right knee. Every time I played a game I was conscious of the knee and worried that I would get a kick on it that would do some irreparable damage. The club had arranged for me to have an operation, but until then I was to carry on playing.

The game was a dogfight. Chester were uncompromising: they had come to Old Trafford and shut up shop, hoping that by packing their defence they could prevent us from scoring and catch us on the break. The tactic almost worked, and in the end we were happy to come off the field having won by the odd goal in three. No-nonsense tackles were interspersed with late and high tackles that verged on the violent. All through the game I was worried about being caught by a high tackle on my knee and it affected my concentration and, of course, my game.

That day Chester fielded a wing half called Peter Hauser, who, to be frank, had a good game and showed he could play a bit. But his tackling was hardly full of bonhomie and on several occasions he caught one of our lads with a late or high one.

The referee was John Pickles from Stockport, who, whenever he awarded a penalty, would stand midway between the penalty spot and the goal-line with his back to the player taking the penalty. He did this so that he could listen for the sound of boot hitting ball whilst watching the goalkeeper to see if he moved before the penalty was taken.

The second half was only minutes old when I received a pass from Bobby Charlton out on the right wing. Turning, I skipped past Chester's Ian Metcalf and cut inside towards the goal at the Stretford End when suddenly I was sent sprawling by a tackle from Peter Hauser that took me out just above the knee. John Pickles blew for the free kick and started to retreat towards the Chester goal. I followed and took up a position on the edge of the penalty box. Just before Paddy Crerand took the kick I turned to Pickles. 'He's been doing that all game and he's been getting away with it,' I said, referring to Peter Hauser. 'As for that last tackle on me, why you didn't book him I don't know.'

Without looking at me, Pickles told me he didn't think Hauser's tackle on me was high.

'Well, it sounded high,' I said as Paddy pumped the ball forward.

From the free kick the ball went out for a Chester goal-kick and as I trotted back to the halfway line I mentioned to Nobby Stiles that I didn't think I was getting any protection from the referee and that if this sort of tackling carried on, it could do some permanant damage to my right knee before the forthcoming operation.

Nobby told me not to worry. He had seen the late and high tackles on me and would be sorting out one or two people. Five minutes later, the Chester full back, Roy Jones, brought the ball out of defence and played it just in front of Peter Hauser for him to run on to. Normally it would have been a decent enough pass

– a player would be expected to make the five or six yards to the ball with ease and progress further up the field. Unfortunately for Peter, he was about the same distance from the ball as Nobby.

Peter took off after the ball and at the same time Nobby took three of four strides and launched himself into the tackle. He sailed through the air with his right leg extended like the jib of a crane. Peter got his foot behind the ball at exactly the same time as Nobby's tackle hit the ball from the other side. The laws of physics took their course. As both players made powerful contact from opposite sides, the ball distorted into the shape of a rugby ball before shooting off like a bullet from a gun.

There was the terrible sound of boot on bone as Nobby's momentum carried him straight through and past Peter Hauser.

The ball out of play, referee Pickles immediately called the Chester trainer on to the field to attend to Peter Hauser, who was writhing and moaning on the ground.

The trainer applied a cold sponge to his ankle and asked him how it felt.

'The pain is excrutiating,' Hauser said, grimacing and gritting his teeth.

Nobby Stiles, standing over his stricken opponent, was not in the least impressed. 'Excruciating?' Nobby said incredulously. 'You can't be that badly hurt if you can think of a word like that!'

41

Sound Advice

EVERYONE who was around in 1966 to witness England's World Cup victory over West Germany will have their own special memory of the game. Geoff Hurst's shot coming down off the bar for England's controversial third goal; Kenneth Wolstenholme, commentating for the BBC, telling the nation that 'some people are on the pitch because they think it's all over', and then uttering the immortal words. 'It is now!' as Geoff Hurst blasted England's fourth in their 4–2 victory.

One of the moments that sticks in my memory is my Manchester United team-mate Nobby Stiles dancing a jig around Wembley, holding the World Cup aloft, his unrestrained smile showing the world that his teeth had gaps the size of dominoes.

As I have mentioned elsewhere, Nobby was the most happy-go-lucky player we had at Manchester United – in fact I would go as far as to say that he is one of the most irrepressible people I have met in my life, always smiling, always warm and endearing. Yet that affectionate and bright persona hid the fact that little Nobby Stiles, all five feet five inches of him, was one of the hardest players in the game in the sixties and early seventies.

When people used to say to me that Nobby lacked the skill of players such as Bobby Charlton and myself, or the distribution of Paddy Crerand, I used to point out that Nobby was a naturally two-footed player. He could kick an opponent equally hard with either foot. Nobby had a tackle like a sledgehammer. For all his bad eyesight, once he fixed an opponent in his sights, he never failed to make contact with his prey. But that is not to say Nobby couldn't play to a high standard.

When England played the highly talented Portuguese in the semi-final of the 1966 World Cup at Wembley, England manager Alf Ramsey gave Nobby perhaps the most important role he ever had as a player: man-marking the great Eusebio. The 1966 Portugal side were largely made up of a Benfica team which had, up to that point in the sixties, reached four European Cup finals, winning two of them. Portugal played in a very similar fashion to Benfica – they were adventurous and loved to attack.

Cavalier and highly improvisational, the man who made Portugal tick was their midfield playmaker, Eusebio. Every attack seemed to stem from him and finish with him unleashing one of his thunderbolt shots. Alf knew that if England were to reach the World Cup final, someone had to stop Eusebio playing. That someone was Nobby.

England beat Portugal 3–1 and from start to finish, Nobby followed Eusebio everywhere. By just getting a foot first to the ball as it was played in to Eusebio, Nobby prevented him from displaying his considerable skills and exercising his usual authority on the game. No matter how great a player you are, you can't do it if you haven't got the ball. That night, Nobby was Eusebio's shadow. Everywhere the Portuguese maestro went, Nobby followed. After the game, as the players took to their respective dressing rooms, a tearful Eusebio turned off the corridor to the loo. Nobby, also feeling the need, did likewise. Eusebio turned to see who was behind him and groaned when he saw it was Nobby. 'Even when I go to piss?' he asked agonisingly.

Nobby did a fine job that night. Because Eusebio played it fair, so did Nobby. But when an opponent started the rough stuff, you could always depend on Nobby to finish it. As I've said, the Leeds United side Don Revie put together in the mid-sixties were a very good footballing outfit, but the black mark against them was that they were also one of the dirtiest teams ever to play in the First Division.

Football is a physical game and I took probably more than my fair share of knocks. I never got uptight about it because I accepted good, hard tackling as part and parcel of the game I played. That Leeds side, however, were over the top. The midfield contained three players who thought nothing of kicking anything that moved. Johnny Giles, Billy Bremner and Bobby Collins were all under five feet seven, but big trouble on the park.

Johnny Giles was stylish and a great passer of the ball, and not given to 'mixing it' as much as his two midfield colleagues. Billy Bremner had a shock of ginger hair and was more rugged. I used to call him 'the worry with the ginge on the top' because he was a constant threat to your well-being. By far the most ruthless, however, was Bobby Collins.

Bobby was only five feet four inches tall. We used to joke in the United dressing room that he was the only player in the League who had to have turn-ups on his shorts, but for all his diminutive size, he was a tough nut on the pitch. Bobby had made a name for himself as a hard-working midfield player with Celtic and Everton before moving to Leeds in 1962.

United travelled to Elland Road in the 1964–65 season. Leeds had won the Second Division Championship the previous year and when they stepped up into the First Division they ruffled everyone's feathers as they fought their way up the League ladder. It was my first visit to Elland Road. I knew it wasn't going to be a garden party, but I didn't expect it to be like fight night at Madison Square Garden, either.

As the two teams walked down the tunnel at the start of the

game, I felt a terrific pain on my right calf as someone kicked me with mule force. I turned. It was Bobby Collins. 'And that's just for starters, Bestie,' he said.

From the kick-off it was mayhem. Leeds came at us like something possessed, kicking and hacking any United player who got in their way. For the first ten minutes you wouldn't have thought there was a ball on the pitch. Only twelve minutes had gone when Bremner brought me down for the umpteenth time. As referee Arthur Luty struggled to impose his authority, I decided I was going to try to give as good as I got.

From the free kick our right half, Paddy Crerand, lost possession when Leeds full back Paul Reaney confused Paddy's right kneecap with the ball and decided to hit both. As Paddy lay poleaxed, the ball broke to Billy Bremner. I set off in pursuit and gave Bremner a taste of his own medicine by dumping him on the cinder track that encircled the pitch.

Bremner rolled about clutching his shin. I stood up, feeling well pleased with myself, but spotted Denis Law striding towards me with a face like thunder. 'You stupid prat, George!' he screamed.

'What's up with you?' I asked, not understanding why he was so riled.

'It's bloody well open warfare out here as it is,' Denis said, crimson-faced, 'and now you've gone and upset the bastards!'

The first half progressed they way it had begun. Some of Bobby Collins' and Billy Bremner's tackles were outrageous and a threat to a fellow pro's livelihood. Collins patrolled up and down our right-hand side, dishing out one crude tackle after another. After I had been sent sprawling by a tackle that caught me somewhere around the midriff, Billy Bremner came and stood over me. I thought at first he had come to see if I was OK. Not Billy. 'You'll have to hit Bestie again,' he said to Collins. 'He's still wriggling!'

As I dusted myself down, Nobby Stiles appeared by my side.

'Don't worry, George,' he told me. 'I'm going to put a stop to this nonsense. Forget about Collins, I'll sort him out for you.'

Leeds came on the attack down our right side and their left full back, Willie Bell, threaded a ball down the line for Bobby Collins to race on to. As soon as Bobby latched on to the ball, Nobby took off. He looked straight through the Leeds number 8 as if his eyes were transfixed on some object beyond Collins' right shoulder. When Nobby launched into a tackle, it was like a heat-seeking missile locating its target. The effect was uncannily similar, too.

There was a sickening sound of bone on bone. Above the roar of the crowd, someone was heard to squeal. Bobby Collins was flung through the air like a paper bag in the wind. He went one way, then the other, before being flattened against the concrete wall that separated the fans from the cinder track and pitch. Quick as a flash, Nobby was back on his feet and over by a motionless Collins. Every time you come down our right-hand side and kick George, you filthy bastard,' Nobby warned, 'I'm going to friggin' well hit you like that, only harder.'

Collins struggled to his feet and turned to referee Arthur Luty. 'Did you hear that, ref?' Collins said, pointing an accusing finger at Nobby. 'He said he's going to do me every time I come down their right side!'

'Well, if I were you, Bobby,' Luty said, 'I'd stop going down their right-hand side as from now.'

42

The Night We Won
The 1966–67 Championship

MATT BUSBY tells trainer John Aston Sr to answer the knock on the dressing-room door. A white-coated steward appears and hands John a dozen or so West Ham programmes. John thanks him and puts the programmes on the physio bench that stands in the centre of the Upton Park changing room.

We all reach forward to take one of the small claret and blue programmes. On the cover is a photograph of Geoff Hurst with a caption saying he is the country's leading goalscorer in the 1966–67 season to date with thirty-six goals. Inside is a piece written by the West Ham manager, Ron Greenwood, entitled, 'Will The Championship Be Decided Tonight?'

'They've spelled my name wrong again,' says Tony Dunne, looking at the page featuring the teams for the game. 'They never put the "e" on the end of Dunne.'

'Remember the Aston Villa programme? It ended your surname with a "c" and an "e".' says Denis Law.

Tony turns Denis's words over in his mind until he works it out. 'Like hell did they, you cheeky bastard,' he says.

Denis laughs out loud.

I ask Matt if he knows the referee. Matt looks in the programme. Yes, he does. George Pullin from Bristol. Nobby Stiles thinks it is the same guy who refereed when we lost 2–1 at home to Leicester City the previous April – incredibly, the last time we lost at home. Matt says he thinks that was Jack Taylor from Wolverhampton.

David Sadler, playing as a centre forward, is the first to be ready. He goes into the shower room and starts juggling a ball from foot to foot. John Aston Sr finishes rubbing Bobby Charlton's legs with liniment and moves on to Alex Stepney's back. Alex tells John his shoulder is still a bit stiff after he fell awkwardly against Sheffield United. Bill Foulkes is padding his ankle with cotton wool. Tony Dunne is putting vaseline on his eyebrows to stop the sweat running into his eyes during the match. Denis asks why he bothers. 'You've never worked up a sweat all season,' jokes Denis. Tony tells him to go forth and multiply.

There's another knock on the door. Paddy Crerand opens it. A different steward appears. He is also wearing a white coat. 'Two choc ices and four cornets, please,' says Paddy to the steward.

The steward asks if the players would like sandwiches in the dressing room after the game or want to wait until they come into the players' lounge.

'Bloody sandwiches? At a time like this?' says Matt, annoyed.

Paddy tells the steward to bring the sandwiches to the dressing room. Matt tells Paddy to lock the door and not to answer it for anyone. 'No one! Do you hear?' he says sharply.

Paddy says he does hear and locks the door, muttering that someone else can sit by the door next time, as he can do without this hassle.

The dressing room is hot and the smell of liniment is so strong it's getting on everyone's chests. 'Well this is it,' Matt says, and everyone quietens down to listen to the boss. 'Liverpool. I don't think they have a realistic chance of catching us. Only Forest can do it, but not if we win tonight. And we can beat this lot tonight, can't we?'

We all nod our heads. There's a knock at the dressing-room

door. Matt groans. He doesn't look at Paddy Crerand, but holds out his left hand at a right angle and points at Paddy with his index finger. 'Ignore it!'

We all look at Paddy, who nervously smiles like a schoolboy warned by his headmaster.

'As we all know, these guys can play lovely football. They like to knock it around and they knock it around well – if you let them.' Matt pauses. There is another knock on the door. He pretends he doesn't hear it and continues his talk. 'But we're not going to allow them the time to do that tonight. I want you running at them, harassing them. Don't give them a second on the ball. Knock them out of their stride. Let us dictate the game tonight. I want to see them chasing so much that Moore and Peters come off that pitch at the end breathing through their arses!'

There is another knock on the door. Somebody outside is whispering through the door jamb. Paddy Crerand bends his head to listen.

'. . . so let's take the game to them. Each and every one of you must win your personal battle with your opposite number. Do that and the game and the Championship will be ours.'

Paddy Crerand, who has been waiting for an opportune moment to interrupt Matt, nervously raises his hand as another knock is heard. 'What?' an irritated Matt asks Paddy.

Paddy tells Matt that it is the chairman, Louis Edwards, outside. Matt admonishes Paddy for not telling him sooner and orders him to open the door immediately. As he unlocks the door, Paddy mutters to himself that this is definitely the last time he will sit next to a door.

Louis Edwards steps into the dressing room. He wishes us all well. We thank him. As the chairman prepares to leave the room there is yet another knock. 'It's like Picca-bloody-dilly station in here,' Matt growls as he throws his programme down on to the physio's bench in frustration.

The referee enters and asks all the players to display the studs on their boots. Usually, a referee will go from player to player rubbing the palm of a hand across his studs to make sure there are no jagged edges that can cause injury. We all raise our feet as if the referee is about to hoover under our seats.

'OK, lads, thank you,' he says after a cursory look around the room.

'Call that an inspection?' says Nobby. 'I hope he's more meticulous in his refereeing.'

'Meticulous?' repeats Denis. 'That's a big friggin' word for a Wednesday, isn't it?'

Matt tells us all to be patient if a goal doesn't come our way early on. He tells Bill Foulkes and Alex Stepney to make sure it's kept tight at the back. 'If we're into the last ten minutes of the game and we still haven't scored, don't worry. Be patient, it only takes a second to score a goal.'

The buzzer that indicates it is time for us to take to the pitch is sounded. Everyone stands up. Boots are stamped on the ground. Wilf McGuinness stands by the door to hand out half sticks of chewing gum to those who want them. Matt Busby tells us all to go out and enjoy ourselves and reminds us to take the game to West Ham. We file past him and he pats each one of us on the back. I am the last player to exit. As I walk down the corridor I hear Matt speaking to Jimmy Murphy, Wilf McGuinness and John Aston Sr.

'Well,' he says with a sigh, 'that's another one we've prepared and sent out.'

It's a warm, late April night in east London. The atmosphere is so thick with expectancy and emotion I feel I can reach out and grab a piece of it. Ten minutes into the game, Bobby Charlton gives us the lead. After half an hour that lead is increased when Paddy Crerand pops up in the West Ham penalty box to score.

In the second half two goals from Denis Law and one each

from Bill Foulkes and I give us a 6-1 victory and the First Division League Championship. It is the biggest away win of the season in the First Division.

As we come into the dressing room, Matt is beaming from ear to ear and hugs each one of us as we enter. Everyone is shouting and whooping. Hands dive into the complimentary crate of lemonade.

Denis is having some fun at Paddy's expense about his lack of speed and his goal, claiming that the only reason Paddy was in the penalty area when I crossed the ball was because he was still there from our previous attack. Paddy tells Denis to go forth and multiply.

'I keep telling him to do that,' Tony Dunne says to Paddy. 'But Denis just won't listen.'

A case of champagne has appeared. Wilf says it is from the West Ham directors. Matt tells Wilf to remind him to write a thank-you letter when he gets back to Old Trafford. There's a knock on the door, but no one is bothered or agitated now. The chairman and his co-directors enter. They're smoking cigars the size of rolling pins, all smiling and emotional.

Denis pours champagne from a bottle over Bobby Charlton's head. Bobby laughs. I take alternate swigs from a bottle of bubbly I'm sharing with Nobby Stiles. Alex Stepney asks what's in the sandwiches. Bill Foulkes says it's crab paste and tells Alex they taste 'bloody terrible'.

'They probably got the stuff from the chemists!' jokes Alex. David Herd and young John Aston are singing and shouting. Tony Dunne is crying. Shay Brennan bangs out a calypso rhythm by knocking two lemonade bottles together. David Sadler shakes then pops the cork on another bottle of champagne and sprays everyone in the room as if he were a Formula One racing driver. The dressing room is literally bathed in celebration.

Louis Edwards has found his way to Matt Busby and extends

a hand. 'Congratulations, Matt,' says the chairman. 'A wonderful achievement.'

'Thank you, Mr Chairman,' Matt says softly.

Jimmy Murphy calls for order; the chairman wishes to say a few words. Order restored, chairman Louis Edwards delivers a short speech saying how proud he and his co-directors are of Matt, his back-room staff and the players. He ends by telling us how privileged we are as players to play under Matt, who, he believes, is not only a great manager, but a great man.

'A truly great man,' Edwards reiterates as he concludes.

Matt is encouraged by everyone to say something. He begins by thanking the directors for their support and backing. '. . . And from the bottom of my heart I would like to thank all you players,' he says. 'And may I remind you, as I am sure my wife would if she were here, that in life, there are no great men – only men.'

43

A Turf Moor 'Mare

BURNLEY were a footballing force to be reckoned with in the sixties. As far as we at United were concerned, a match against the claret and blues was one of our biggest games of the season. The fixture had added spice in that it was considered a 'derby match' and consequently had a highly competitive edge to it. I always enjoyed playing against the men from Turf Moor. In the sixties, the teams included the likes of Adam Blacklaw, Jimmy Adamson, Brian Miller, Ray Pointer and Gordon Harris and in the seventies, Frank Casper, Martin Dobson, Paul Fletcher and – as Denis Law used to call them – the Battling Baldies, Ralph Coates and Peter Noble. When United met Burnley, the fans were always assured of a game in which the level of skill and entertainment would be out of the top drawer.

In those days, teams would play one another twice in the space of as many days over the Christmas and Easter holidays. I can readily recall us being on the wrong end of a 5-1 Yuletide scoreline at Turf Moor, only to reverse that scoreline when we played at Old Trafford a couple of days later.

There were no easy games for us at that time. Every game United played was a big game: partly because the crowds would roll up and the opposition would raise their game because of who we were; partly because the First Division at that time had strength all the way down to its basement. Teams such as West Bromwich Albion, Sunderland, Newcastle United or Leicester

City were just as capable of giving us a good game as Liverpool or Spurs – somewhat different from today's Premier League, where, with the exception of five or six teams, the standard of football is very mediocre.

Although Burnley were never a 'big club' in terms of money or attendance figures, they were big in footballing terms. They had a superb youth system that was a conveyer belt of good young players which, combined with some shrewd purchasing by manager Harry Potts, ensured they always had talent a plenty.

As the sixties closed, United visited Turf Moor early in the season for a midweek game. The evening was as warm as a sunned cat. Burnley didn't boast the largest of stadia and as we ran down the tunnel I remember glancing up at the heaving terraces. It seemed that everyone was packed in so tight there was hardly the width of a fag paper between them.

Those few moments before the kick-off were when I used to feel the butterflies. Impatient for the game to start, I'd feel the need to be totally comfortable in order to perform well. I'd have one last adjustment of the tie-ups; ensure that the socks were folded over at the top exactly the way I liked them to be; laces done up just so. I'd get rid of the chewing gum, because if I swallowed it whilst I was running and breathing heavily, I could choke and my mother would say: 'I told you what would happen. But would you listen? Oh no. Not you.'

The last tune I'd heard playing on the radio on the team coach would run through my mind and I wouldn't be able to get rid of it. Bobby Charlton would turn towards me, clap his hands and say, 'Come on George. Let's get at these right from the start.' I'd nod. Bobby would then turn his attention to the defence. Then I'd start breathing the tune I'd heard on the coach. Funny that. It only happens when you play a game, breathing a tune. I wonder why?

I'd just begin to think that my shirt wasn't tucked into my shorts properly when the referee would blow his whistle and immediately all those random thoughts would disappear, like rain falling on an ocean.

The game against Burnley started like all the other games against them: at a frantic pace, with the ball flying from player to player like a pinball and Matt Busby shouting from the dugout for Bobby to 'put a foot on it and slow it down'. In the opening minutes, Denis Law, like a kamikaze pilot, hurled himself between Blant and Nulty to head narrowly wide from my cross. At half-time he told me the quality of the crosses I was putting into the penalty box was on the slide. Two of the six I had made came across with the the ball's valve facing him when he headed it.

Burnley's young Steve Kindon unleashed a thunderbolt from thirty yards. Alex Stepney never moved as it hurtled narrowly past him and wide. In the bath after the game, Nobby had a go at Alex about it, saying it was a wonder Alex never caught pneumonia from the draught the ball made as it flashed past him.

For some inexplicable reason, there are games when you have an off day. You try one or two things and they don't come off. It affects your confidence and you end up giving a performance that's well below par. Worse than that, there are those occasional games where you feel you can never put a foot right. Everything you do is wrong and the harder you try, the worse it becomes. That night against Burnley, John Fitzpatrick was having such a game.

With about fifteen minutes gone I had managed to get behind the Burnley back four but as I cut inside from the wing I saw their 'keeper, Harry Thompson, covering the near post and Mick Docherty coming across. Aware of John Fitzpatrick breaking from midfield, I simply rolled the ball back into his path. Nine times out of ten, John would have put a chance like that away. On this night, however, he nearly knocked the hands off the town hall clock. A gap suddenly appeared

212

halfway up the terraces as fans ducked to evade his still rising shot.

Ten minutes later, I sent a ball deep to the far post. Denis Law was there, hanging in the air as he often was, and he headed the ball down towards John, standing on the edge of the six-yard box. To this day I do not know how he contrived to miss. Six yards from goal, John's shot was so feeble Harry Thompson collected it on the fourth bounce.

We told John to get his head up and not to worry, but those two misses affected him. His distribution then started to suffer. Soon John couldn't have made a decent pass if he had seen a teenage nymphet in a swimsuit. The further the first half progressed the more his game deteriorated. His ball control got so bad his second touch was a sliding tackle.

John, being the player he was, tried to rectify the situation by trying harder and putting himself about more. It was all to no avail. That night the gods had conspired against him. They had deemed that John Fitzpatrick would, in footballing parlance, 'have a 'mare'.

With half-time approaching he was desperate to avenge himself. I had cut inside and laid the ball off to Denis some twenty-five yards from the Burnley goal. Denis looked up and saw John in amongst the Burnley defenders facing him and carried the ball forward looking to play a wall pass. Now, a 'one-two' is a useful way of bypassing defenders, but it is dependent on the quality of the return pass from your team-mate. Knowing what sort of game John was having, perhaps Denis should have thought better of attempting a 'one-two' with him, but hindsight, as they say, is a wonderful thing.

Laying the ball off to John, Denis carried on the run he hoped would take him past a square-looking back four. He had expected the ball to appear on the grass in front of him so he could take it on in his stride. Out of the corner of his eye, he saw a ball coming to him – at rocket speed and heading for his throat.

To give Denis credit he made a valiant effort to get the ball under control. In mid-stride, he swivelled his hips and did something I had never seen anyone in football attempt before – or since. He tried to control this wayward bullet of a pass with his chin.

If the pass had been good, Denis would have taken the ball on and probably scored. But his momentum had been halted as he attempted to get the awkward rocket pass under control and I can still vividly recall the tackle that hit him. It was one of Doug Collins's more humane tackles. It took Denis out at about thigh level.

As Denis limped away following treatment, he turned and offered John a look like Clement Freud sucking on a lemon whilst a steamroller runs over his foot.

With the score at 0–0, only minutes remained of the first half when I managed to shake off a couple of shadows. Looking up, I saw John taking up a good position running into the box and sent the ball across so he would meet it in the air goal-side of the penalty spot.

This was purely tactical on my part, because Harry Thompson, although a very competent 'keeper, was not the most adventurous. In fact, Denis and I used to call him 'Crocus' because we reckoned he only came out once a year, and then only briefly. But Harry came off his line that night, all right. In fact he left it like a sprinter would his blocks, hurling his considerable frame through the air and punching the ball so high we lost it in the glow of the floodlights. It was a punch any top heavyweight would have been proud of. It carried on after it had connected with the ball and met an airborne John Fitzpatrick smack in the face.

John went down like a bag of hammers. No amount of smelling salts or water could bring him round. He was out so cold I thought Wilf McGuinness and Jimmy Murphy would have to lift him on to the stretcher with ice tongs.

Denis and I were the first into the dressing room at half-time. John, dazed and groggy, was sitting slumped at the far end of the room, flanked by Wilf and the club doctor. Grabbing teas from the tray we went over to ask how John was faring.

'Not too good,' the club doctor informed us. 'He's regained consciousness, but his memory has gone. He doesn't even know who he is.'

Denis studied the situation for a moment and took a sip of tea.

'Tell him he's Pele!' he told the doctor.

44

Vision of Europe

MORE things are wrought by prayer than this world dreams on, so the saying goes. In 1968, Manchester United and our worldwide network of supporters and admirers realised the power of that belief when we followed in the footsteps of Celtic to become the second British club to win the European Cup.

On the night of 29 May 1968, millions of people entreated the gods to look favourably upon United in our quest for the European Cup, particularly so for Matt Busby.

United had rebuilt following the Munich disaster. The Busby Babes of 1958 had been superseded by other babes, and those by even more babes. Three European Cup semi-finals had been lost, in 1957, 1958 and 1966. That warm May night at Wembley in 1968 saw the realisation of a dream.

As a player, I have always been one for the big occasion. Matt Busby told me that his definition of a great player was someone who had great games in the great games. He then, very kindly, told me he believed I was in that category. The fact that it was my mentor who told me this and not some football pundit made me feel very proud, yet very humble.

If the players wanted to win the European Cup that night for anybody, it was for the boss. In the fifties, when UEFA instigated the competition, Matt saw its potential straight away. When the Football League learned of Matt's enthusiasm for European competition their response was, quite simply, pathetic. Matt was warned of the repercussions he and United would face if this 'gimmick' competition distracted them from their domestic programme. A little pressure was put upon the great man by the League's administrators to 'forget the idea'. Matt, however, stuck to his dream of Europe. He was one of the first people involved in domestic football to perceive that the game was going to change irrevocably.

England's 6-3 humiliation at Wembley in 1953 and their 7-1 defeat a year later in Budapest against the same Hungarian side told Matt that the balance of power was shifting away from the British game. The 'foreigners' hadn't just caught up; they were overtaking. There were exciting new coaching techniques. The old 'W' formation was becoming old hat on the Continent. People were experimenting with new patterns of play, different formations, and they were proving highly effective on the football field. A new type of football game was emerging.

It had been Matt Busby's vision that European competition should develop and grow. Above all, he wanted to win the European Cup, not just for United, but to prove that British football was back as a force once more. That night at Wembley against Benfica, I think we did that.

There was no long, involved team talk prior to the game, no detailed analysis of the opposition. In fact, I can recall the very words of Matt's team talk that night: 'Go out and enjoy yourselves, boys.' That's all he said, and indeed, needed to say. There's a lot of claptrap written and said about what makes a good football manager. The truth of the matter is it's easy to be a good football manager. All you have to do is sign good players. And that is the hardest part. Matt Busby, however, did that. Consequently, he didn't have to tell the likes of Bobby Charlton, Nobby Stiles or myself what to do out on the pitch. We were a team in every sense of the word, and we played as one that night. Young Johnny Aston had the game of his life on the left wing. Brian Kidd, on the day before his nineteenth birthday, showed a maturity far beyond his years in deputising for Denis Law. Alex Stepney was superb and the boys in front of him outstanding.

When the final whistle blew and we had won 4-1 in extra time, I looked across and saw big Bill Foulkes and Bobby Charlton, both of whom had been with Matt almost since they had learned to kick a ball, in tears. I'm sure the nation shared their weeping and their joy, and more to the point, fully understood why they reacted the way they did.

Even though the game went into extra time, we knew we were going to win it. That side had character, on the pitch and in the dressing room. It was larger than life. And the biggest character of all was Nobby Stiles.

In addition to being known as Nobby, Stiles had two other nicknames in the United dressing room. Happy, because no one had ever seen him other than full of joy and smiles, and Clouseau, because of his constant stumbling and fumbling, which was due to his terrible eyesight. On the night of the final against Benfica, Nobby marked Eusebio out of the game, just as he had two years earlier in the World Cup semi-final against Portugal. The amazing thing about it is that Nobby managed to track this great player throughout the match when, compared to him, Mr Magoo would enjoy twenty-twenty vision. Contact lenses were, at the time, crude and the ones Nobby wore were like the clear glass saucers that accompanied a cup of espresso. As Paddy Crerand used to say, 'There can't be much wrong with your eyesight, Nobby, if you can see through those lenses.'

Such was the discomfort in wearing those lenses that Nobby could not bear to keep them in for any length of time. It led to one of the most amazing incidents of that European Cup final. During the dressing-room celebrations following our win, Nobby realised his spectacles had gone missing. Having worn his contact lenses for the entire game, he could not face any further discomfort and therefore decided to do without at the post-match celebration dinner back at our hotel.

The players and club officials sat down to dinner, the European Cup taking pride of place on the top table. This table formed the head of a 'T' shape, with the players and their wives and girlfriends occupying a long table set at a right angle to it. I sat at the very end, next to Denis Law, with Nobby opposite. Midway through the dinner, Nobby excused himself and headed off to look for the washroom.

Ten minutes or so must have passed before I expressed my concern about Nobby to Denis. Since Nobby was the most accident-prone person we had ever met, I suggested to Denis we went off in search of our maladroit mate.

The washroom was empty. The lobby receptionist was adamant no one had passed her. We searched the lounge and cocktail bars without success. We were making our way back to United's private dining room when we happened to pass another room in which a dinner was taking place. The sign outside said it was a Rotarians Charter Dinner and, as we looked through the half-open door, we could see a 'T' shaped table arrangement similar to ours. At the end of the table sat Nobby, quietly helping himself to someone else's main course.

Few Rotarians noticed Denis and I sprint into the room and drag away a totally bemused Nobby.

Years later, there was an extraordinary footnote to this incident. I attended a sporting luncheon in Hertfordshire, and as I sat chatting with one of the top-table guests, United's winning of the European Cup was mentioned. 'The strange thing is,' said my companion, 'I attended a Rotary dinner the night you won the European Cup and it must have been the wine or something, but when I looked across from where I was sitting on the top table, I could have sworn I saw Nobby Stiles dining with us.'

He shook his head, questioning his own judgement. 'I was *sure* it was Stiles,' he said. 'Only it couldn't have been, could it? Besides, when I looked across a little later, he had gone.'

45

Chelsea at Home

1969–70

BILL FOULKES walks into the home-team dressing room at Old Trafford and makes for his usual seat in the far corner. Bill always helps himself to tea from the large brown metal teapot sitting on the physio bench, but not today. He's sporting four stitches in his bottom lip, a legacy of the game against Everton on Wednesday night.

'How's the mouth?' asks Tony Dunne.

'She's at home with the kids,' quips Bill.

Denis Law is brushing his left boot with a small black brush. 'Did I tell you I've had a final demand from the tax people, George?' he says.

'No. How much?' I ask.

'Eight hundred and fifty friggin' quid,' says Denis, brushing with more gusto.

'What have you done about it?'

'I wrote them a letter,' says Denis.

'Saying what?'

'Saying I couldn't remember borrowing it from them!'

A wave of laughter washes around the dressing room.

'How did you know it was a final demand?' asks David Sadler.

'When I opened the front door this morning it was pinned to the door with a dagger,' says Denis.

More laughter.

'For Christ's sake don't make me laugh,' Bill Foulkes mumbles.

Wilf McGuinness, who has taken over this season as manager from Matt Busby, enters the room. He asks everyone to sit. He begins by telling Jimmy Ryan he is not in the side today and thanks him for coming into the team on Wednesday night and doing such a good job against Everton's Jimmy Husband. 'You did great, Jimmy, son. Couldn't have asked for more from you,' Wilf tells him.

'Aye, but I'm dropped today,' Jimmy says under his breath as he stares down at his feet.

Wilf continues. 'So Brian Kidd comes back. Kiddo, you know what I want from you? Just keep making those runs in their box. Like we did in the shadow play in training.'

Wilf announces the team. 'OK, lads.' I want you ready in fifteen, then we'll have a little natter.'

He helps himself to tea and exits from the room. Shay Brennan, wearing only his underpants, moves the teapot from the physio's bench and climbs on to it face down. He immediately shouts out in pain and pulls himself up on one elbow, rubbing his chest with his left hand.

'Ye daft bugger, you've just lifted the teapot off there, you should have known it would be hot,' says old Jack Crompton, the physio. He pushes Shay back down on to the hot vinyl bench cover and starts to press fingers the size of bananas into his shoulders.

'Had one today?' Tony Dunne asks me, referring to a bet.

'No, didn't bother, Tone.'

'I bumped into Mick Summerbee this morning. He was on his way to join the Man City coach. They're at Arsenal. He gave me a tip in the three-fifteen.'

'Summers gave you a tip?' says Denis. 'He couldn't tip a cup of tea over!'

Nobby Stiles is in agreement. 'Summers gave me a tip at Kempton last week. Dead cert, he said,' Nobby tells us wistfully. 'It fell in the bloody paddock.'

'Gerraway wit' you,' Tony says.

I slip off my shoes, then my trousers. I fold my trousers over my arm and turn to place them on the hanger on my peg.

'What the 'kin' hell are those you're wearing?' screams John Fitzpatrick, pointing to my underpants.

'Present off a girl admirer,' I tell him.

Fitz comes across and starts to pull at my underpants. I tell him to leave me alone. The underpants are white with small red hearts. Fitz won't let me be until he's found out what the girl has written in biro on the fly. Knowing I won't get any peace until I let him see, I allow him to pull me around so he can read the inscription. '"Put my friend Rumpleforeskin in here! Can't wait till I kiss him again!"' Fitz shouts the message at the top of his voice, then shrieks with laughter. 'I don't believe it! Which slag sent you those?'

'Your missus,' I say to shut him up.

I change, but leave my socks around my ankles in readiness for Physio to rub embrocation into my legs. He comes and kneels in front of me, takes my right leg and places my boot in his groin. The embrocation is cold on my legs. 'You could at least have warmed your hands, Jack,' I complain.

'Stop being a big baby. You're like sulking Sam over there,' Physio says, nodding in the direction of Jimmy Ryan, who is sitting in a corner looking forlorn.

'Jimmy did all right on Wednesday night,' I say quietly.

'He did,' Physio agrees. His hands knead and rub my calves as if they were baker's dough. 'But as soon as Kiddo was pronounced fit, Jimmy was out. Kiddo is Wilf's favourite, you know that.'

'You reckon?' I ask, having seen no evidence of this myself.

'Way Wilf sees it, Kiddo's got eyes bluer than a cross-eyed joiner's thumb.'

Physio finishes off my legs with a slap and moves across to Brian Kidd, who is calling for him.

'Great to see you back in the side, Kiddo.' Physio says. 'You've done well, because Ryno can do little wrong in Wilf's mind.'

Bobby Charlton comes over to me. His face is strained and concerned. 'You watch out for Ron Harris today, George,' he says as I tie my stockings with strips of bandage.

'Why?'

'Because I know what he's like. When it's a line ball he'll come across and hit you around the waist and try to send you flying into the concrete wall. He doesn't give a toss what he does to you.'

'Well, if he tries that with me when the ball is played down the line, you know what Harris can expect?' I say.

'No. What?' Bobby asks, impressed.

'As much bloody line ball as he wants.'

Bobby doesn't seem to see the joke and returns to his seat. He looks as if he's about to face a firing squad.

Wilf McGuinness returns and gives a short talk about what he expects from us today. He doesn't spend much time talking about our opponents, Chelsea, preferring to extol our own virtues and strengths. 'Paddy,' he says, attracting Paddy Crerand's attention. 'Your pace is deceptive.'

'True, he's even slower than he looks!' pipes up Denis.

Everyone laughs. Even the corners of Bobby Charlton's mouth turn up a millionth of a millimetre.

'Paddy,' Wilf continues as the laughter subsides. 'Your passing is so sharp we could open tin cans with it. Keep threading those balls through for George to run on to. Just make sure George is involved, plenty. OK?'

Paddy nods.

'Bobby, I don't have to tell you what to do. You know what

you have to do out there today. Just sit in and get forward when we break, like you've been doing.' Wilf goes around the room in this manner. Giving gentle reminders of what is expected and offering his own inimitable brand of confidence-boosting psychology. 'George, son. Brilliant on Wednesday night. I'd play you with your overcoat on . . . John Aston! You're looking sharp. You look strong, fast – in – fact you'd beat pigeons if you raced them . . . Denis, a lot depends on you today. You gave Lawson in the Everton goal too much time and space on the ball on Wednesday night. He had time to shit, shower and a shave by the time you arrived. I want you in that box. Attack the space. Always be expecting the unexpected, because there'll be a time when their 'keeper, Bonetti, will drop the ball, and when he does I want to see you there to get it . . . OK, lads? Good. Now go out there and express yourselves. Enjoy yourselves. Remember – nothing is work unless you'd rather be doing something else. So let's get out there, do the things we're good at, and we'll end up with two points. Then we can all enjoy our pint tonight – and George his ten!'

We make our way down the tunnel. Just as we reach the point where the massed ranks of the terraces will catch their first sight of us, Denis Law peers around the ground. 'What would you all say to Bestie lending me his E-Type for tonight. Good idea?' he says as he runs out into the daylight. A deafening roar from the crowd greets us. 'Well, sounds as if they're all in agreement with that!' says Denis with a cheeky grin.

Chelsea prove difficult opponents. They have a highly gifted and creative midfield that includes Alan Hudson, Ian Hutchinson, Peter Houseman and Charlie Cooke. Up front are Peter Osgood and Tommy Baldwin, both players capable of making you pay heavily for an error. The defence is formidable: David Webb, Mickey Droy and Ron Harris make their considerable physical presence felt. It's as if the Kray brothers have given their wholehearted support to whatever Mozart and Michelangelo can produce.

Deep into the second half of the game, Paddy Crerand threads a ball down the line and I'm away. Ron Harris, the Chelsea left back, comes to force me further out wide. I don't want to go that way. I drop my right shoulder. He goes to my right, I go to my left. Peter Houseman comes across. I slow down my pace and just as he comes alongside me and thinks he has the measure of me, I accelerate away.

Looking into the middle of the park I see Bobby steaming up the pitch. He's some forty yards from the Chelsea goal. I know he can hit them with thunderbolt force from around thirty and what's more get them on target. As Ian Hutchinson comes snapping at my heels, I lay the ball back for Bobby to run on to.

Bobby in full flight is a sight to see. He's like a thoroughbred gliding the last few yards to win the Ascot Gold Cup. Before he makes contact with the ball he glances up at the Chelsea goal and I know he's picked his spot. He doesn't break stride as he latches on to the ball. His right foot carries through and his right shoulder is over the ball as he hits it in the sweet spot. The ball leaves his boot like a bullet leaving a gun barrel.

It's heading for the top right-hand corner of the net. There's a green blur as Peter Bonetti in the Chelsea goal gets airborne. As he flings himself outwards and upwards his arms seem to grow in length. The crowd roars, 'Go-aww!' as Bonetti, in mid-air, clutches the ball in both hands.

He hits the dirt by his left-hand post. His eyes close momentarily as mud sprays and he clutches the ball to his chest. Bonetti opens his eyes and sees a pair of boots inches from his face. His eyes move upwards. There is a pair of red stockings. He then notices the knobbly knees and legs as white as the shorts they protrude from. There's a red shirt, the cuffs of which are pulled over the palms of the hands and gripped by the finger tips. Denis is grinning like a Cheshire Cat. 'I'm here again,' he tells Bonetti, 'and if you don't let go of it next time, it'll be your fucking head I'll put in the back of the net!'

We race back towards our halfway line but the expected clearance doesn't come. Bonetti is shaken by Denis's promise and slices his kick. It lands on our left-hand side, level to the centre circle, in the Chelsea half. Sensing an opening, I sprint across to our left wing. Glancing up I see Ron Harris moving in for it too. We both have about the same distance to cover to reach the ball, but I fancy my chances.

I reach the ball first, flick it forward with the outside of my right boot and just as I'm taking to my toes, Harris's tackle hits me. It's lower than usual, just above knee level. I crash to the ground as a searing pain shoots down the right side of my knee.

Old Jack Crompton has tottered out of the dugout, sprayed the knee with PR spray to deaden the pain, washed my face with a sponge and shuffled back into the dugout before Paddy Crerand has sprinted the ten yards to see if I'm OK.

The referee, having taken Ron Harris's name (did he really have to ask?), retreats towards the Chelsea goal in readiness for the free kick to be taken. I'm standing over the ball with Paddy. 'I'll have this one,' Paddy says.

I step back a few paces to give Paddy the room to put the ball wherever he has a mind to. With the inside of his right boot he rolls the ball the yard to where I'm standing. Quick as a flash the Chelsea midfield move in to deny me space. I can't hang about so I take off down the left-hand side. John Hollins is the first I confront. I flick my hips and drop my left shoulder, Hollins slides under me and I'm away. Ron Harris again. I send him one way, then the other. He's still standing, and between me and the goal. I feint to the right but swerve to my left. Ron has gone off somewhere to my right, it's a dummy so good sniffer dogs wouldn't find him.

I'm at the angle of the penalty box and looking up. All I can see is a wall of blue shirts. In the gap between Alan Hudson and David Webb I see that Peter Bonetti has come slightly off his line to cover his right-hand post. With the toe of my boot I flick the ball up off the ground to around knee level, get my right boot underneath it, my head over it and lob it towards the far corner of the net to Bonetti's left.

Some blue shirts turn to see where the ball has gone. Some join Bonetti in backpedalling to try to clear it. Peter Bonetti is the nearest to the ball, but not near enough as it drops under the bar and into the far corner of the net.

The ground is filled with noise. It's as if 63,000 people have just simultaneously received the news that they have each won a jackpot on the pools. I'm too knackered to run so I just turn around with my right arm held aloft, Bobby Charlton appears from nowhere and flings his arms around me. Suddenly Denis is there too, rubbing the palms he's been spitting into all afternoon through my hair. I'm almost bent double from the weight of team-mates as they jump in the air and descend on my back and shoulders.

As Chelsea kick off to restart the game, Paddy conveys the message he's had from the dugout. 'Eight!' he shouts across to Kiddo and I, referring to the number of minutes remaining. 'Let's keep it nice and tight. Don't let them back into this.'

Back in the dressing room at the end of the game everyone is elated but too tired and weary to be buoyant about the win. The atmosphere is strangely subdued. We all look over the cuts and bruises we have acquired and slowly recover from the rigours of battle with tea from the big brown pot.

'You got the money to pay the tax people?' I ask Denis.

'Aye. I'll raise it somehow,' he says nonchalantly, but I detect his furrowed brow.

I'm towelling myself off and hoping Denis is not going to let the tax thing get him down.

'They were a hundred and ten pounds each, you know,' Denis says as he buttons his shirt.

'What were?' I haven't a clue what he's on about.

'King Kong's bollocks!'

The dressing room returns to normal as laughter rings out around the room.

46

Non-Stop Flow

I n 1979, Hibernian contacted me and asked if I would like to go and play for them. I was out of football at the time and the offer was a good one. I was to be paid £1,000 a match, on a game-by-game basis, and was to be allowed to do some of the training in London and fly up to Edinburgh on a Friday for matches.

I enjoyed my spell with Hibs. Though their fans never saw the best of Best, I'd like to think I gave them one or two memories. They certainly gave me a few.

I made my debut for Hibernian at St Mirren on 24 November 1979 and the attendance of 14,000 was double their average home game. We lost 2–1, but I did have the satisfaction of scoring the Hibs goal. When I made my home debut at Easter Road, 21,000 turned up to see us beat Partick Thistle 2–1. The attendance for the previous home game against Kilmarnock had been 7,000, so I felt I was good value for money simply from the extra revenue I was generating from the increased attendances.

In January 1980, there was another large attendance for the home game against Celtic. The game ended in a 1–1 draw and once again I managed to get myself on the scoresheet. The sky was battleship grey and a north-easterly wind made the air as crisp as new banknotes. Matches between Hibernian and Celtic are always closely fought affairs and this particular game was no exception. Celtic had in their team that day a player called Murdo MacLeod who was having a running battle with our Ralph Callachan for the domination of the midfield.

There are a lot of footballers who are what I call instinct players. It's as if the pass or the shot they produce is the product of some innate ability that does not require thought. MacLeod and Callachan were above that. They had the ability to read a game, evaluate it and change it on the spot.

When Callachan received a pass, he'd buzz about the field with the ball held at his feet as if by a magnet. He would prompt and probe the Celtic defence in the hope that it would crumble. By shifting his shoulders to his left or right he'd sway like a bird on a twig before high-stepping over flaying boots. On any other day, Ralph Callachan would have dictated the course of the game, but today he was up against an inspired Murdo MacLeod.

There are some players who hardly ever speak on the pitch and there are others who never seem to shut up. Murdo MacLeod belonged to the latter category. Short and stubby as a hedge fence, MacLeod bellowed instructions and commands to his Celtic team-mates from the moment the referee put his whistle to his mouth. 'Give me the ball.' 'Off you go.' 'Back you come.' 'Drop in.'

Throughout the first half MacLeod never stopped shouting. What was more, every time there was a corner, free kick or goal-kick, he was there to verbally contest it by taking issue with the harassed referee.

I went down heavily following a tackle from Celtic's Roy Aitken. Roy's studs had caught my ankle and the pain was searing. 'Nothing wrong with him, referee. He's playing for sympathy,' said MacLeod.

Our trainer pointed to my blood-soaked, ripped stocking. 'Wash it in clean water,' MacLeod told our trainer, John Lambie. 'Then dry it. Get some lint and put some anti-septic on it. Press it against the wound and then wind a bandage around the ankle, making sure you use the heel as a support.'

John Lambie looked up to tell MacLeod he didn't need him to tell him how to do his job, but now MacLeod was badgering the referee about adding time on to the first half for stoppages such as this.

Callachan and MacLeod continued their private battle during the second half with MacLeod's incessant banter forming a backdrop to the game. 'Does he ever shut up?' Ralph Callachan asked me as we stood together when play was held up whilst a Celtic player received treatment.

'Apparently not,' I said as MacLeod offered advice to the referee on how he could be paying more attention to what was happening on the field.

'How can he run around the way he does and never stop mouthing?' Ralph wondered out loud. 'He must have lungs the size of mailbags.'

There were only minutes remaining of the game and both sides were locked together at 1–1 when MacLeod and Callachan contested a high ball. Callachan took off from the ground a little late and as a consequence did not time his jump to get maximum height. MacLeod was already heading the ball upfield when Callachan came up alongside him and took the full force of his right elbow in the side of the head. It was an accident, but Callachan fell heavily. He lay prostrate on the turf, knocked out colder than the January air.

From MacLeod's header the ball had gone out of play and the referee immediately blew for John Lambie to rush on with his medical bag. John's head had hardly poked out of the dugout before MacLeod positioned himself over Callachan, congratulating the referee on calling a halt to the game so promptly. 'This looks like a serious injury and one can never be too careful where injuries to the head are concerned,' he lectured as the referee's eyes started to glaze over.

As John Lambie knelt over Callachan he received a running commentary on what he should be doing to revive his player. 'Wash his face before using any smelling salts. Make sure the face is dry before you use the salts, though. Otherwise, if he snorts water up his nostrils, it could panic him.' MacLeod hardly paused for breath.

A few of the Hibs players, myself included, had come across to see how Callachan was.

'You lads had better stand back a couple of paces,' MacLeod told us. 'In his condition he needs as much air as he can get.' He looked at me. 'If you really want to help, George, you could undo his laces and take his boots off. That sometimes helps if someone is unconscious.'

Just then there was a moan and a murmur as Callachan started to come back to the land of the living.

'He's obviously responded to those smelling salts,' MacLeod told John Lambie. 'What you should be doing now is thinking about getting him back on his feet.' He continued his non-stop flow of advice as Callachan blinked, opened his eyes properly and turned to John Lambie with a look of total bewilderment on his face. 'For God's sake, somebody hit me again,' Callachan winced. 'I can still hear him!'

47

The Curtain Rises

C OME mid-June, football fans eagerly await the publication of the fixtures for the forthcoming season. Immediately they look for four things: who their team is against on the opening day of the season; who they play on Boxing Day; when the derbies take place against their arch-rivals; and who they meet on the final day of the season, just in case they're involved in a Championship or relegation that goes to the wire.

The quality of the opposition on the last day is important. Just how many fans over the years have seen 'Liverpool away' at the end of their fixture list and said, 'Well, if we are involved in something at the end of the season, let's just hope to God it's resolved before we have to go to Anfield'?

On the opening day of a season, players, like the fans, are as hopeful as a spring morning. By 4.40 p.m., many are resigned to another season of uphill struggle. Yet, irrespective of how they fare for the rest of the season, I have noticed that promoted clubs invariably get a result on the opening day. It didn't bother me too much who United had for their first game, but I always preferred to avoid a promoted club. They pull out all the stops because they're in a higher division and want a good start to boost their confidence. Furthermore, promoted teams are always a bit of an unknown quantity.

On a trip to Glasgow some time back, I bumped into one of the greatest footballers Scotland has ever produced, genial Jim

Baxter. We talked football and I mentioned my theory about promoted clubs doing well on the opening day. I was surprised to hear that Jim had noticed it too. 'That's right, Bestie,' he told me. 'If we had a newly promoted side at Ibrox on the first day of the season, they always did well. They'd restrict us to five goals or sometimes just the four.'

It may be many years since anyone last called him Slim Jim Baxter, but I had to spend only a few minutes in his company for the years to roll away and to be reminded of that very special Baxter magic.

Jim started his career with Raith Rovers but in 1961 joined Rangers, where he won every honour the Scottish game could offer. I played against him in internationals, but it was when he came south to sign for Sunderland in 1966 that we got to know one another better.

Jim was an artist on the field. When Scotland were beating England at Wembley in 1967, he took off down the left wing and juggled the ball from one foot to the other as if he were having a fun kickabout in the local park. On another occasion in that game, he reached the byline and crossed the ball by turning side-on to the goal and kicking with a right foot that came from behind his left leg. Two audacious displays of skill – and in front of 100,000 people in an international match.

Three months later, Jim was selected for the Rest of the World team to play England at Wembley, rightly taking his place in a team which included Alfredo Di Stefano, Ferenc Puskas and Eusebio.

There are those who say that Jim may well have been an artist on the football field, but he didn't have appetite or driving ambition; that win or lose, Jim's state of mind was the same. Those people obviously don't know Jim, or what happened after the opening game of the 1964–65 season.

The previous season, Rangers had swept the domestic honours board clean. The treble of League Championship, Scottish FA

Cup and League Cup came to Ibrox. Their reserves won their respective League and Cup, as did their youth team. Come the start of the 1964–65 season, hopes were high for a repeat performance. Morton, who had been runaway winners of the Second Division the previous year, were early-season callers to Ibrox. It was a game Rangers were expected to win handsomely, but that day, they were a fixed-odds punter's nightmare. Morton ran out 2–0 winners.

Jim Baxter dragged his weary limbs out of the bath and was making his way back into a disconsolate and silent dressing room when a cheery and happy-go-lucky George McLean swept by him. Big George was the Rangers centre forward, a player who relied on instinct, natural talent and brawn rather than brain. This was the player who, on returning from a European Cup match in Spain, was asked by Customs if he had anything to declare. 'Aye, as it happens I have,' said Big George earnestly. 'After last night's game I got my leg over, but what has that got to do with you?'

Jim Baxter stood dumbfounded at the sight of Big George. Everyone else in the dressing room was devastated at the defeat they had suffered, but here was the centre forward chirpy and chipper as he would be after a 4–0 victory. George stood before a mirror, in slacks and white shirt unbuttoned at the collar. He combed his hair diligently and whistled a carefree tune as he did so, unaware that all eyes were looking at him disapprovingly.

'Have you no shame?' Jim asked. 'We've just been beaten by a team we should have wiped the floor with. There were forty-five thousand folk out there who paid hard-earned money to watch us. And we turned in a performance that was utter rubbish!'

It was as if Big George hadn't heard a word Jim had said. He just continued combing his hair and whistling to himself in the mirror.

'Did you hear what I said, George?' Jim continued in slightly raised tones. 'We were crap out there today and what you've got to feel so happy about, I don't know, because you were the bloody worst!'

Still no reaction. Big George continued to comb and whistle merrily. 'How you can stand there so happy beats me!' Jim said, becoming angry. 'Your performance today was a bloody disgrace. You went out on to that park and strolled about. You turned in the biggest heap of crap I've ever seen from a pro footballer! The biggest load of crap, do you hear me?' Jim spat out his words with fury.

Suddenly Big George stopped combing his hair and turned towards his accuser. 'Aye,' George said knowingly, 'and there's plenty more where that came from!'

. . . And Now

'Some so-called open minds should be closed for repairs.'

Ken Bolam, composer/musician.

'Success is getting what you want, happiness is wanting what you get.'

Rodney Marsh

48

TV-AM

In 1980 my life was going nowhere. Mary Shatila, my partner, was yet to come along and give my life meaning and purpose. I had checked into the Vesper Hospital in California to be treated for alcoholism. They were the first tentative steps I took to get my life back on the rails.

I was in a bad way, and on returning to England received an invitation to appear on TV-AM, one of Britain's first breakfast TV programmes. The programme was doing a tribute to me and Denis Law. Michael Parkinson and Jimmy Greaves were already in the studio when I arrived, ready to make their own personal appraisal of my playing days. Soon my old team-mate Shay Brennan turned up. I was touched because he had flown across specially from his home in the Irish Republic to be with me.

Although from the outside I looked OK, inside I felt awful. There must have been telltale signs in my behaviour because Jimmy Greaves, who had been through alcoholism himself, confronted me. 'Are you OK?' he asked.

'Not really,' I told him.

Greavsie disappeared and returned with a mug of black coffee, laced with a very large brandy. He knew that I was using drink as a medicine to calm me down and there was a long road ahead of me before I would be able to confront life without it.

Those were dark days, but even then there were humorous moments and lessons to be learned. That day on TV-AM there were both. The tribute over, I was sitting on the sofa alongside Shay Brennan when Anne Diamond, one of the show's presenters, welcomed the next studio guest, the Spanish singer Julio Iglesias.

After his introduction, Julio began to talk about his career as a singer and revealed that prior to becoming the heart-throb of millions of women worldwide, he had in fact been a footballer. He told us he had been a goalkeeper and at one time had a spell with the great Real Madrid, though he never played higher than the reserves.

I was still in a bad state and was uncomfortable about being in the public eye for so long when I was feeling so dreadful. What was more, at that point Shay Brennan and I were sitting like statues, making no contribution to the programme whatsoever. I began to grow anxious and wanted to race out of the studio for fresh air, but obviously I couldn't. I felt trapped.

Julio sat relaxed and bronzed like some Greek god talking of his lifestyle in Spain. Suddenly he mentioned the word, *mañana*. Anne Diamond, obviously in tune with the TV-AM viewers, jumped in. 'Just for the benefit of our viewers who don't know,' she said to Julio, 'can you explain what the Spanish mean by the word *mañana*?'

Julio gave us a smile that looked like the keyboard on a Steinway. He leaned back on the sofa, crossed his legs to reveal a pair of patent leather shoes that Des O'Connor would have killed for, and with a laconic wave of his right hand began to explain. 'In Spain,' he said, his voice lazy and laid-back, 'the word *mañana* means maybe the job will be done tomorrow, maybe the next day, maybe the day after that. Perhaps next week, next month. Next year! Who cares?'

Anne Diamond saw this as an opportunity to bring Shay and I into the conversation and immediately turned her attention to us. 'Now, George, you are from Northern Ireland – Shay, you live in the Irish Republic. Do the Irish have an equivalent for the word *mañana*?'

Shay Brennan leaned back on the sofa and slowly crossed his legs as he had seen Iglesias do. 'No,' he said, hand waving lazily in the Spanish style. 'In Ireland we don't have a word to describe that degree of urgency.'

It was the relief I needed. I convulsed with laughter and felt much better.

From that day on I realised the true worth of laughter. When you're down and dispirited it's the only tonic. Nowadays I get by without a drink for weeks on end, but I always try to have a good laugh every day.

49

Lawman

DENIS LAW has been a great friend to me. When we played
together at Manchester United he was part of what the
press called the 'Holy Trinity' of Best, Law and Charlton. I'll
reserve judgement on myself, but for me, Denis Law and Bobby
Charlton are two of the greatest players there have ever been –
not only in the British game but in world football. Both played at
the very highest level and both performed brilliantly even when
the opposition they faced was top class.

People have said – and somewhat unkindly, I might add
– that Bobby and I have never got on. They say it without
consulting Bobby or me. The truth is that we do get on and
always have done.

If you look back at any photographs or film recordings of when
we played in the sixties, you will notice that the first person to
be there to congratulate Bobby when he scored was me and
vice versa. During the Championship year of 1967–68 it seemed
that every Sunday the newspapers would carry a photograph of
Bobby and I hugging each other after one of us had scored a
goal. It became such a regular occurrence that on one occasion,
after Bobby had scored the only goal in a 1–0 win over Spurs,
as we threw our arms around each other I said jokingly, 'We're
going to have to find some other way of meeting, Bobby. I think
your wife is beginning to suspect!'

We have respect for one another, but we have never socialised because we have always lived different lifestyles. At United in the sixties, Bobby would finish training and go home to his wife and family. I was single, however, and having no such responsibilities would head off in search of my idea of a good time, which was any female between sixteen and fifty-five whose legs started just below the neck and who had enough sex appeal to stampede a businessmen's lunch. In those days I was the young man about town.

Bobby is somewhat reserved, and whilst he is always polite, he can appear dour at times. Denis Law, however, brings the party with him. Denis is a bubbly man, always ready with an anecdote or a quip. His coiffured blond hair has hardly changed over the years. He exudes warmth and always sports a cheeky grin that makes you constantly think he must know something you don't.

He has never shied away from putting his point of view across if he felt it right to do so and a couple of years back he really ruffled the feathers of a young presenter from BBC Radio. Denis had been working on a local BBC station in the north-west providing expert analysis of a United home game. Following the results and reports at five o'clock, the presenter wanted him to come back on air and answer some hard-hitting questions about football.

With minutes to go to this live broadcast, the rookie presenter started to get cold feet about the content of his interview in case Denis said something that landed them in hot water – or worse still, with a legal writ. As they prepared to 'go live' the interviewer asked Denis to use the word 'allegedly' if he referred to anyone or anything even marginally controversial. Denis agreed, but this did little to allay the anxieties of the programme's host. 'I don't want you to mention any names,' he told Denis.

Denis rocked back in his chair and offered one of his cheeky grins. 'Well, how can I talk about what the people in the game are really like if I can't mention their names?' he asked incredulously.

The presenter, one eye on the studio clock, was thrown into a panic. 'We'll use spoonersisms!' He said excitedly, happy with himself at having arrived at a solution. 'Yes, that's it!' He reiterated to a disbelieving Denis. 'When you refer to a manager or player and it's going to be a controversial answer, swap the first letter of the surname with that of the Christian name and vice versa.'

Stifling his laughter at the absurdity of the situation, Denis had no option but to go along with it as only seconds remained before they went live on air.

'So Kenny Dalglish will be Denny Kalglish, Brian Clough is Crian Blough. OK?' the presenter said, one eye on the studio, 'On Air. Light.' the light turned to red and the interviewer introduced Denis and informed the listeners that they were about to be treated to a hard-hitting, no-holds-barred look at football, warts and all. However, such was the nature of the programme that in certain circumstances it would be necessary to refer to names by way of a spoonerism to avoid possible legal action.

The show had been underway for some time and was progressing nicely, when the presenter started to talk about deviousness in football management. 'In your view, are there devious people in football management today?'

'Yes,' Denis replied in honesty.

'Who's the biggest?'

'The biggest devious bastard?' Denis asked in confirmation.

'To put it that way, yes,' said the presenter, nodding to indicate that Denis should use the spoonerism.

'George Graham!' said Denis as the interviewer turned three shades of purple.

246

50

The Coach

A T the close of the 1991–92 domestic season, Denis Law
and I flew out to Australia to fulfil a contract to coach
young players. We were working just south of Sydney in New
South Wales, at a Soccer School of Excellence which had been
up and running for about three years. Aussie youngsters would
spend anything up to a fortnight there and the classes ranged
from simple basics for the very young to the improvement of
individual skills for older kids.

Football may never be as popular as cricket Down Under,
but it does have a tremendous following and it is, I am
happy to say, growing. As far as I could determine this
is down to three factors: better coaching and promotion
of soccer at the grass-roots level; a solid following amongst
immigrants from such countries as Italy, Greece and Vietnam,
who have formed strong and prosperous communities; and the
success of the national side, which just failed to qualify for
the 1994 World Cup finals by being pipped by Argentina in
a two-legged play-off.

Denis and I had been contracted to coach at the school for
four weeks. On our first morning we were getting changed into
our tracksuits when we overheard a group of young Australian
boys having top fun at the expense of one of the coaches at the
school. From what we could gather from the conversation, the
coach, like ourselves, had just arrived on a short-term contract.

It was obvious that the poor guy had quickly become the butt of everyone's jokes.

'Tell you what we should do,' I heard one of the boys say. 'We should ask him to run with the ball.'

Great howls of laughter.

'I saw him walking across the playing fields this morning. He was waddling like a gander. He's too bloomin' fat for soccer,' said another voice.

'Fat!' someone else shouted, laughing to himself. 'He's the only guy I've ever seen put on a tracksuit and fill it!'

More shrieks of mirth.

'Come on, you guys,' another voice said. 'He's coaching us today, let's try and get the fat bastard to run. Bet you his body would still be jogging ten minutes after he stopped running.'

Uncontrollable laughter galed from out of the room next door. Denis and I counted our blessings. Neither of us fancied being that coach with those boys, on this or any other day. As the hilarity subsided, a deep booming voice cut the air. 'You lot can laugh, but I don't think it's funny at all.'

At first Denis and I thought the coach had a sympathiser, but the booming voice told us otherwise.

'Our parents have paid good money for us to come here and the school appoints a fat slob like him. What the hell has he been able to teach us about football?'

Mutterings of agreement.

'Yesterday's session was a disgrace,' Booming Voice informed the room. 'We can't understand him because his English is so bad, and looking at him he can't have played soccer at any standard. He's a tub of lard!'

The room agreed, and what had started out as harsh but humorous remarks about this poor guy had turned decidedly nasty. I feared for him.

One of the school's administrators arrived and called the youngsters out on to the playing fields. Denis went off to join the group of boys he had been assigned to. I wasn't due to take a class until early afternoon, so, having the morning free, I decided to walk around the playing fields to get a feel for the place.

It all seemed very well organised. Small groups of boys and girls were divided into age groups and taught a variety of skills. Each had a ball and I couldn't help but think how fortunate they all were. The quality of life for these youngsters was wonderful. Here they were learning the beautiful game under turquoise skies at a school which could boast facilities as good as those at Lilleshall, where England train.

It was a far cry from where I first learned the game on the streets and in the back lanes of the Cregagh Estate in Belfast. In those days to own even a plastic Frido ball was to have a popularity amongst boys normally reserved for our true heroes, such as Davey Crockett or Dick Barton. The boy who owned a ball called all the tunes. If he thought his shot was a goal and you were certain it had passed over the pile of coats that served as a post, you conceded the goal. If you didn't, he'd pick up his ball and head for home. It was as if you were playing with some crazed dictator who had to be constantly humoured.

In those days, I supported Wolves and at Christmas would receive a new pair of boots which I couldn't wait to put on. Wearing a yellow shirt, which was the nearest I could get to the old gold of Wolves, black cotton shorts and grey school socks with two green hoops on the fold at the top, I'd race out of the house on Christmas morning.

'Who are you today?' my dad would ask.

'Johnny Hancocks,' I'd tell him, imagining I was the tricky Wolves winger before dashing off to see if Napoleon had got a new ball for Christmas.

As I circled the lush playing fields of the coaching school I counted six classes taking place. On the far side I came across a class which I thought had been divided into two groups. It was only when I got nearer that I realised the reason for the schism. One group had broken away from their coach and were whiling away the morning aimlessly kicking a ball about amongst themselves.

As I approached, the coach was holding a ball under his arm and trying to put a point across to the knot of youngsters who were kicking their heels before him. He didn't seem to be having much success.

He didn't look like anyone's idea of a sporting type: a large man verging on the obese, his hair oilier than a car mechanic's rubbing rag and swept back over his forehead. His cheeks were flabby and grey and contrasted sharply with the tanned, fresh faces of his charges. A considerable belly pushed the elasticated waisteband of his tracksuit bottoms to breaking point.

As I approached, a little buzz went around the group and I heard my name being mentioned as the boys turned away from their coach to take a look at me. I smiled at him and nodded towards a bag of footballs to see if it was OK with him to take some. He offered a smile in return that seemed a mixture of embarrassment and relief, indicating I should go ahead.

Emptying the sack of balls on to the emerald green turf I called the rebel group to me. With the class again united I then laid out ten footballs in a line, some twenty-five yards from goal. 'I'm going to ask Coach to kick the balls from here and try to hit the crossbar. How many hits do you think he'll get?' I asked of the group.

Shoulders were shrugged and feet were shuffled before Booming Voice spoke. 'One! Even he has got to have a bit of luck going for him,' he said, pointing an accusing finger at Coach.

I invited the coach to have a go. He waddled up to the ball. Glancing up, he measured the distance, leaned deftly to his left, brought his left foot parallel to the ball and with his right gently chipped the ball forward. The trajectory was a perfect parabola. The ball made a slight chinking sound as it danced on top of the crossbar.

Having the distance measured and knowing what amount of weight to put behind the ball, the coach drove the second ball with force. The ball was still rising when it buzzed the crossbar like a tuning-fork. With his following eight strikes, the portly coach hit the crossbar every time. The youngsters stood slack-jawed in amazement.

I retrieved one of the balls and chipped it to Coach. He controlled it on his chest and it immediately fell under his spell at his feet. He lifted the ball on to his right foot, then changed it to his left, effortlessly continuing this for some thirty seconds before trotting away towards the goal. On his way, he deftly bounced the ball on his right foot. For the return journey, he juggled it on his left. Not once did the ball touch the ground.

When Coach got back to us, I extended the palm of my right hand to indicate he should continue as he pleased.

He nodded his appreciation and started to juggle the ball on his right foot before flicking it up in the air. He leaned forward and the ball came to rest on the back of his neck. Flexing his neck muscles, he flipped the ball into the air once more and proceeded to play head tennis with himself.

Tiring of this display, he dropped his head slightly, an action which made the ball come to rest on his forehead. It stayed there for a few seconds. Again the neck muscles twitched and the ball took to the air.

The youngsters started to cheer and whistle their approval as Coach took the ball first on his knee, then, boot at a slight angle, on the side of his heel. He then started to juggle and bounce it on the back of his boot before once again flicking it high in the air.

'Issa goal!' he shouted as the ball began its descent. Body over the ball he volleyed it from fully thirty yards towards the goal. It nearly ripped the net off. The youngsters cheered and clapped their hands in enthusiastic appreciation.

I smiled at Coach and raised a hand to indicate I was leaving him to it. With a dignified smile, he placed his head to one side and give a single, gentle nod of thanks. I was about to walk on when I heard a familiar voice. 'That was brilliant, Coach!' Booming Voice said. 'Who are you? We don't even know your name!'

I swung around to confront him. 'To you,' I said sternly, finger wagging, 'He's *Mr* Puskas.'

Yes, the chubby coach was none other than Ferenc Puskas, the brains behind the wonderful Hungarian team who, in beating England 6–3 at Wembley in 1953, inflicted England's first defeat by a foreign side on home soil. He played in the fantastic Real Madrid team that won the European Cup five times between 1956 and 1960 and to my mind still deserves considerable respect for the true footballing genius he was.

51

Cheers!

MY problems in the past with drink have been well publicised. It was a tough battle to get my drinking under control and having done that, I don't intend to take a backward step. There was a time around 1984 when I could have drunk myself into oblivion and, more to the point, not cared. Now things are different. I still like the odd drink or two, but these days I get my work done first. I've never been so busy. Writing books, appearing on TV and radio, speaking at sporting dinners, theatre tours, coaching young players – there is hardly a free moment in my diary.

In 1987 I met Mary Shatila, and she changed my life. Mary is my common-law wife, my lover and best friend, my confidante and my strength. She handles all my business affairs, acts as my manager and agent, and without doubt, as those who are close to me know, I owe all of what I am today to Mary. I was talking to my good friend Rodney Marsh and told him I wished I'd met Mary years earlier than I did.

'But the point is, you did meet her,' Rodney said. 'Some people go through life and never find the right partner. You have.'

'But I had to go through a lot of bad times before Mary and I found one another,' I said.

'True, but without the rain there is no rainbow!' he said.

*   *   *

Now I can joke and recall the funny stories from the days when booze was my partner. For amidst all the sorrow and depression of such times, there were still humorous moments.

One night Kenny Lynch, the singer and entertainer, and I staggered out of Slack Alice's, the night club I owned in Manchester. I felt so bad, I couldn't even make it to a taxi and I sat down on the edge of the pavement outside the club in the hope that the night air would make me feel better. Kenny came and sat next to me. After a minute or two we were joined by a young policeman.

I was aware of him looking at me, but I couldn't move because I was so drunk. After a while the young bobby crouched down next to me. 'I'm taking you in, you're drunk,' he said.

'He's not that drunk,' said Kenny. 'I've just seen his fingers move!'

In 1982, my old United team-mate Denis Law was worried about how much drink I was tucking away. He bought me one of those audio cassettes that are supposed to help you give up drink by subconsciously relaying a message whilst you sleep. On the cassette a soothing soft voice told me I would feel better without booze. As the message was relayed, soothing music and the sound of either a seashore or tropical rainstorm could be heard in the background.

About a month after Denis had given me the cassette I met him at a sporting dinner and he asked me if the cassette had been any help.

'As a matter of fact it has stopped me drinking,' I said. 'Only whilst I'm asleep, but it's a start.'

Nowadays there is still the odd occasion when someone will ply me with drink, and I will lower my guard and go over the top. That happened before the *Wogan* show on BBC Television in 1991.

Wogan, as I'm sure you'll remember, was a chat show in which Terry Wogan would interview two or three star personalities and reveal aspects of their career, usually in a humorous vein. The series was broadcast live in the early evening to a peak-time family audience but it was really, in a production sense, cheap television. The guests were paid around £150 for appearing and few interesting or funny anecdotes were ever revealed – usually the guests were there solely to promote their latest book television series, film or record. With the benefit of hindsight, I can look back at my appearance and ask why I had been invited. After all, I had no book, video or television series to promote.

As soon as I arrived in the Green Room, which is where the guests assemble before a show goes on air, I was plied with drink. No sooner had I finished one than another was thrust into my hand. I could have refused, of course, but once a drinker gets a taste, the old weakness resurfaces. When the time came for me to appear on the show, I was the worse for wear to say the least, and all the hard work and denial of the previous years had been undone in an instant. Inebriated and slurring my words, I did my worst in front of millions of TV viewers.

The next day, nearly all the morning papers ran the story: there were photographs of me on the show, comments from BBC personnel – clearly the BBC publicity and PR machine had responded remarkably quickly.

Close friends believed I had been set up. They felt the BBC had staged the incident to get publicity for a series that was not doing as well as they had hoped. The BBC denied this, stating that they would never pull such a cheap stunt and didn't need the publicity as *Wogan* was doing very well in the ratings. I had no reason to disbelieve them and just wanted to forget the whole incident. That said, *Wogan* did disappear from our screens, which is unusual when a show is 'doing really well'.

I am convinced that Terry Wogan had no idea what had gone on in the Green Room and, to be fair, I was invited back on to the show at a later date. The BBC were taking no chances then, however – the other two guests were Cliff Richard and Sister Wendy, the art critic nun!

After I had so much bad publicity for appearing roaring drunk on *Wogan*, Oliver Reed and Alex Higgins rang me up and said, 'We don't know what all the fuss is about, George. You looked fine to us!'

In 1988, an old pal of mine from the halcyon days of the late sixties in Manchester, Bobby Deakin, died of cirrhosis of the liver. Bobby was a real livewire. He wheeled and dealed, and in the main worked as a ticket tout in Manchester, buying and selling tickets for the big games at Old Trafford and Maine Road and the rock concerts in the city.

When Bobby had cash on the hip, he'd go out and spend it on a food and drink binge. How his wife coped I'll never know, for sometimes he'd disappear for three or four days at a time. I had been coaching in Australia and only heard of Bobby's passing some two months afterwards. On my return to England, I called to see his long-suffering widow, Mary, during a trip to Manchester.

I paid my respects and over tea she told me about Bobby's final days and how on his deathbed he had questioned her about their fourth child. Apparently, of the four children they had, Bobby had always wondered if the fourth and youngest was his as she was conceived when Bobby was disappearing regularly on benders. 'He made me swear to tell the truth on a Bible,' Mary told me.

'And was he the father?' I asked solemnly.

'Oh yes,' Mary said. 'No question. I swore on the Bible at his bedside that he was the father of our fourth kid, which he was. He died peacefully not long afterwards.'

Mary took another sip of tea and gazed off into the distance. 'Thank God he didn't ask me about the other three!' she said, shifting uncomfortably in her chair.

52

The Passing of a Legend

THURSDAY 20 January 1994 will always be a day I remember with great sadness. It was the day the great Sir Matt Busby passed away. I have detailed elsewhere in this book just what Sir Matt meant to me, but on the day I attended his funeral, my deep sorrow was tempered with many fond memories of the great times I had with Sir Matt at Old Trafford.

There were so many former Manchester United players attending Matt's funeral that we were transported by coaches to and from the service. It was during one of those journeys that one of the most poignant tributes to Matt was paid.

I was on one of the coaches along with the likes of Denis Law and Paddy Crerand. As the coach set off the mood on board was one of mourning. Then Paddy spoke. He remembered the time Denis was having problems in front of goal and had not scored for weeks. We were about to play Aston Villa and Matt told Denis before the game that the Villa goalkeeper, Colin Withers, was related to him. Matt said he had been speaking to Withers' mother, who had expressed concern that Denis might break one of her son's hands with the sheer power of his shooting.

'I've promised her you won't do that,' Matt said. 'So when you score today, Denis, put the ball in the corner of his net out of his reach.'

A ripple of laughter rang around the coach as the players recalled the incident.

Then Nobby Stiles asked if anyone could remember the time Paddy complained that he had been kicked on his funny bone whilst lying on the ground after making a tackle. 'Then just part your hair on the other side. That way it won't show,' Matt told him.

More laughter.

David Sadler recalled the time Denis Law went to see Matt about getting a pay rise for the players and we all ended up getting less money, the story which appears in 'The Professional's Lot'. I recounted Matt's response when Bill Foulkes remarked that Jimmy Ryan did not seem to be as well dressed since he got married three years previously. 'I don't know how you can say that,' said Matt. 'It's the same suit!'

Soon the coach was echoing with gales of laughter as player after player remembered his own personal story of Matt's humour and warmth. To some it may have appeared wholly inappropriate that such frivolity and happy banter should take place on the day of Matt's funeral, but to those who played under him it was a fitting tribute to all the wonderful times we spent with him.

As we travelled on the coach I thought about what Sir Matt used to say when he returned to football after the Munich tragedy of 1958 about the absurdity of the constant pressure placed upon managers and players to win games and trophies when measured against life's true realities as he and others had experienced them that fateful day in Munich. Matt knew how to get matters into perspective, and in so doing he understood power. From the fifties to the day he died, I firmly believe that no one had more power at Old Trafford than Matt, and that includes the directors.

To me, Matt Busby was more than a great manager: he was a great man of football. He managed Manchester United the way, I am told, he played football himself. Thoughtfully, neatly, calmly, cleverly and with great vision, concealing his lack of speed with superb positioning and tactical know-how and, most of all, playing with a great sense of enjoyment and fun. I, like all the other players fortunate enough to have played under him, hold Matt Busby in the highest regard and, like all the others, I too miss him terribly.

No one can measure the loss of one life against another – we should all be considered equal. And yet, on the day of Sir Matt's funeral, I could not help but think of the famous words of George Orwell, that some people are born more equal than others.

53

Simply Red

WHEN Manchester United won the Premier League Championship for the second season in succession in 1994, they emulated the United side that clinched the First Division title in 1956 and 1957. The fact that Alex Ferguson's brilliant team also beat Chelsea 4–0 in the FA Cup final to join Tottenham Hotspur (1961), Arsenal (1971) and Liverpool (1986) as the only teams to win League and Cup doubles this century may well elevate them above all other United teams. That said, the mark of a truly great side, as I am sure Alex Ferguson is only too aware, is to win the European Cup. If Alex and United can go on and do that, no one will be more pleased for them than I.

Such achievements spark off much debate and discussion and I am often asked to compare the United team which won the League Championship in 1993 and the League and Cup double in 1994 with the side I played in, which won titles in 1965 and 1967 and the European Cup in 1968.

I think it's impossible to make indisputable comparisons between the team in which I was privileged to play, which included the likes of Bobby Charlton, Denis Law, Nobby Stiles and Alex Stepney, with the super side created by Alex Ferguson. To begin with the game is very different in the nineties compared to the sixties. It is faster and because it is played at breakneck speed, some of the artistry and subtle skills have gone by the way. That said, the United side put together by Alex Ferguson played exhilarating football which contained plenty of skills to admire.

There was a hard-edged consistency about the 1993–94 double-winning side. Throughout the season they played a total of sixty-three games and lost only six. That sort of record demands respect. Every game was played at high tempo and for Alex Ferguson's United team to display so many skills in the fast and furious modern game is even more to their credit.

The Premier League was in danger of being dominated by teams who favoured the long ball or who were so well organised and efficient that they were bereft of flair and the cavalier spirit. The Manchester United of 1993 and 1994 brought back wonderful entertainment and flowing football as a spectacle and, more importantly, many sides tried to follow suit.

Another big difference between the sixties and the nineties is the strength of the opposition. Look at the Premier League when United won their 1993 and 1994 titles and you won't find more than five or six good football teams of any note. In the sixties, the First Division was much stronger throughout the League – even those teams who spent their lives near the foot of the table were more than capable of giving any other side a good game and playing highly entertaining football themselves. Sunderland had Jim Baxter and Colin Todd; Fulham, Johnny Haynes and George Cohen; Blackpool had Alan Ball and Jimmy Armfield. How many teams in the bottom half or even mid-table in the Premier League can boast top international players?

To compare the United side I played in with the one so brilliantly created by Alex Ferguson is like comparing a ship with an aeroplane. Both are wonderful for getting you where you want to go, but both were constructed for different modes of travel. Sir Matt Busby and Alex Ferguson brought in players because they were capable of doing a specific job within a pattern of play that was designed to win the League in differing circumstances. Both have been highly efficient and entertaining, but it is very much a case of horses for courses.

Sir Matt Busby thought the world of Alex Ferguson. In the last two years of his life, Sir Matt beamed with pleasure and pride every time he watched a game at Old Trafford. He loved the way Alex had the team playing and he thoroughly approved of his style of management. Perhaps Matt saw a lot of himself in Alex and realised that he wanted to play the game the way he liked to see it played: with flair, imagination and style. Alex will never have a greater accolade for his skills as a football manager than the admiration of Sir Matt.

To Alex, Manchester United and all football players and fans the world over, here's wishing you all the Best of Times!